An introduction to

The Commemorative Masonic Order of

ST. THOMAS OF ACON

David Kibble-Rees

"Of this, we, as Englishmen, should be humbly but justly proud. For of all the five noble Orders of Knights, viz. Templars, Hospitallers, Teutonic, St. Lazarus and St. Thomas, this was the only one with an English foundation." (J.E.N. Walker)

Lulu.com

Other publications by the same author:

The Freemasons of Malta 1977 - 1986   1986

A Short History of the Society (The Operatives)   2004

A history of the Worshipful Society of Free Masons,
Rough Masons, Wallers, Slaters, Paviors, Plaisterers
and Bricklayers (generally know as The Operatives)   2006

© 2008

ISBN: 978-0-9559890-0-1

CONTENTS

	Page
The start of things	1
The Order expands	7
Continued expansion	11
The Order today	17
Thomas à Becket	21
The Crusades	27
After the Siege	41
The Order in London	49
In retrospect	55
Knights Humilitas and Knights Caritas	59
Grand officers	60
Grand Preceptors of Provinces	62
Provinces of the Order	63
Chapels of the Order	64
Postscript	66
Index	69

INTRODUCTION

This book has been written for the benefit of anyone with an interest in this unique masonic Order which was founded thirty-five years ago. Those who are members (which includes lady freemasons, who have their own version of the Order) will already have been given a certain amount of historical information during the course of their admission ceremony but, if they are anything like me, that will only have served to whet their appetite for more. My hope, therefore, is that the book will go some way towards satisfying the curiosity of some, whilst pointing others in directions they may wish to travel at some time in the future.

There are four points I feel obliged to make, the first of which is that, although I enjoy my membership of this delightful Order, and will for ever be grateful to the man whose enthusiasm led to its recension, I must remind readers that it is a purely *commemorative* Order, and makes no claim whatsoever to be the linear descendant of the medieval Order from which it takes its name, or any other Order of a like or similar name, either in England or anywhere else. The reasons its founder thought it an Order which *ought* to be commemorated are explained in the first chapter.

Secondly, in the hope that it will make it more readable, I have deliberately refrained from providing footnotes, and have kept references to a minimum.

Thirdly, it is inevitable that in producing any book, there are going to be errors and omissions and, for any of those, I apologize in advance. I can only hope they will be few and far between.

Finally, I wish to place on record my grateful thanks to Andrew Stephenson and Barry Clarke, both of whom helped and advised me during the writing of the book; to Mike Crowson, for his advice and for designing the cover; and to my wife, Margaret, who has always encouraged me and done so much to improve my computer skills although, in the end, it is she who has brought the book to a finished state.

David Kibble-Rees
November 2008

CHAPTER 1

The start of things

Until the end of 2006, when its owner emigrated to New Zealand, 38 Westcombe Park Road, Blackheath, London, was the home of Andrew B. Stephenson, a Christian, author, printer, organist and scholar, who achieved eminence in several Orders of freemasonry, not least of which were the Societas Rosicruciana in Anglia (of which he was Supreme Magus from 2002 until mid-2005) and the Commemorative Order of St. Thomas of Acon (of which he was Grand Master from 1991 until 1997).

It was a large house, and possibly too big for its owner's domestic needs who, at that stage of his life, lived there alone. As a result, he used part as a library, part as an office, a few rooms for accommodating visitors, at least one for dining, and one at the top of the house as a masonic 'temple'. No one who visited it will ever forget the mass of books, papers and artifacts heaped about the building, or the rotary cement mixer and tools which stood undisturbed in the hallway for years as part of a programme of repairs which was never quite finished. Neither will they forget the friends they met there, most of whom were distinguished in various Orders and professions but, above all, scholarly and enthusiastic as far as their freemasonry was concerned. It was, in fact, a small but intense hotbed of masonic hyper-activity!

Andrew's temple was used by a curious mixture of small masonic Orders and societies which he either enjoyed or wished to sustain, including the Fellowship of the Rosie Cross, the August Order of Light, the Martinists, the Spiritual Knights, the Pilgrim Preceptors and, of course, the Commemorative Order of St. Thomas of Acon. There were probably others.

'Acon' (and it is hoped no one will be offended if the Order's name is shortened to that from now on) is a masonic Order which

St. Thomas of Acon

owes its current recension to one man, John Edward Nowell Walker, a former resident of 28 Wathen Road, Dorking who was born in 1901, died at the age of ninety, and was one of those who regularly visited Andrew's temple. He was initiated into Dorking Lodge No. 1149 in 1928 and subsequently joined Waldeck Lodge No. 1969 in 1944, the Lodge of St. Andrew No. 518 (Scottish Constitution) in 1945, and the Lodge of Love and Friendship No. 6123 in 1961. During the course of a long career in freemasonry, he became a member of most Orders including the Holy Royal Arch, Mark, Royal Ark Mariners, Royal and Select Masters, the Allied Masonic Degrees, Red Cross of Constantine, Knights Templar, Knight Templar Priests, Rose Croix, Royal Order of Scotland, Secret Monitor, Operatives, the August Order of Light, the Societas Rosicruciana in Anglia (of which he became Recorder-General), and the Order of Eri (of which he became Chancellor). He also co-wrote a lecture explaining the Royal Ark Mariner Tracing Board, and two books, both of which are available in the library at Freemasons' Hall, Great Queen Street, London; one, a gem of meticulous research, on the history of Mount Sinai Chapter No. 19 (HRA), and the other on the first fifty years of Perram Council No. 45 (Allied Degrees). And it is from those books that we can today obtain the clearest impression of his personality, for in one he describes himself as an indefatigable researcher and founder of Dorking museum', whilst in the other he wrote of himself 'A great lover of London he was admitted to the Livery of the Worshipful Company of Gold and Silver Wyre Drawers in 1960'. In short, he was an enthusiastic and committed freemason, with an abiding interest in research and a life-long affection for London and its history. It is also apparent that he was a man with few illusions for, in the book on Mount Sinai Chapter, he wrote of himself that 'being of a suspicious nature (he) was never successful in life and was greatly detested by his superiors'.

Another interesting, but unconnected, fact concerning Walker, which could easily be ignored but is thought to be revealing as far as his character is concerned, is that it was he who campaigned for a plaque to be erected on the house next door to his own in Dorking, to commemorate the fact that Lord Olivier (the famous actor) had been born and brought up there. Unconnected though it may be, it nevertheless serves to illustrate his obvious belief that achievements in life should not be too easily forgotten which, in the context of this book, is important.

The start of things

Although he earned his living by working in Insurance in the City of London, he made a point of utilising the opportunities thereby presented by spending his lunchtimes carrying out research in the various facilities conveniently at his disposal, which included the Guildhall Library, and it was during one of those visits that he first chanced upon the medieval and apparently long-forgotten Order of St. Thomas of Acon.

There were three aspects of that Order which particularly intrigued him, and these were:

The Order was entirely English in origin, which was unusual as far as the early Crusades were concerned, which mainly drew on the titled families of those areas we would now regard as France, Italy, Germany and the Low Countries. Hence the dominant role of early crusaders, such as Godfrey de Bouillon, Raymond of Toulouse, Bohemond of Taranto, and Baldwin of Boulogne, the first crusader 'King of Jerusalem'.

Secondly, no one ever seemed to want to accept responsibility for it, which he discovered when he encountered the 1510 CE report of the installation of its Master. It appears that, on that occasion, no one could be found who was willing to take charge of the Order, even though its members had all been asked, a situation which was only resolved when the assistance of Dean Colet of St. Paul's Cathedral was sought, he being the Patron of the Order. In due course, the Dean assembled the Knights of the Order and announced that their new Master would be John Yong (or Young) S.T.P., the Vicar of Honey Lane Market. The Vicar had apparently seated himself in the lowest and most anonymous position in the chapel and was so alarmed at his sudden elevation that he would have made good his escape and avoided the responsibility, had not the Marshal and his Deputy seized him before he could reach the door and took him before the Dean who told him, 'You are the Master!', thereby ending the uncertainty which had hitherto existed and reminding the knights of that lesson in humility contained in the Gospel of St. Luke, when Jesus explained 'For everyone that exalts himself will be humbled and he that humbles himself will be exalted'. Not surprisingly, this episode (interpreted somewhat dramatically – as will be explained in Chapter 8) was incorporated by Walker when he came to write the ritual of the Order, and it is today enthusiastically re-enacted annually in every Chapel, as part of the installation ceremony of its Worthy Master, to the

St. Thomas of Acon

unending delight of its members, who generally regard it as one of the Order's most engaging features.

The last of the three aspects which so fascinated Walker were the actual circumstances under which the original Order was formed. These will be described in greater detail later but, for now, it is hoped it will be sufficient to explain that, during the 3rd Crusade, there was a long and bloody siege at the Mediterranean seaport of Acre (or Akko, as it is now known) in the Holy Land. This dragged on for years, and the cost in lives was terrible. More often than not, the injured were simply left to die, and the dead were left to rot. Fortunately someone eventually took pity on the dead and the dying, and that was a small group of English crusaders under a man now known as 'William the Englishman', who decided to do something about it, and went on to form a small - but separate - Order, which came to be known as the Knights of St. Thomas of Acon, who made the distasteful task of burying the dead their principal aim. This was eventually extended to include the ransoming of captives, but more about that later. At this stage it is only necessary to outline the features concerning Acon which John Walker found so fascinating which, to sum up, were the fact that the Order was entirely English; its Masters invariably displayed great humility; and the raison d'etre of its members was their compassion for the plight of the dead, in giving them a proper burial. What followed was that Walker described his discovery to Andrew Stephenson and, between them, they devised a ritual which they shared with a number of others, all of whom - over time - provided additional input, until a workable ritual, based on that of the original Order, was finally agreed. These included:

Desmond Bourke

A clergyman with a voracious appetite for all things mystical, who provided the closing Eucharist, together with an alternative Agape, from the first written account of the Last Supper as it had been translated into English. He also made a point of visiting the church of St. Nicholas Anglicorum in Cyprus, the significance of which will become apparent later, and his photographs of which were incorporated into the ritual. Copies of four of those photographs are now displayed at all meetings of the Order and are regarded somewhat like 'tracing boards'.

The start of things

George Duke
A retired police officer, who was heavily involved in a number of small Orders, and served as Director-General of Ceremonies for the S.R.I.A. He added the rubrics for the floor-work and provided the original coffin used as part of the four candidate's 'tests', which are something else that is distinctive about this Order. He also organised its first pilgrimage to Canterbury. Interestingly, Andrew Stephenson recalls that, in the early days of the new Order, there was no ceremony involved with the pilgrimage, and those members of the Order attending simply assembled in Canterbury and visited the Cathedral as a group.

Michael Penrose
'Pen', as he was affectionately known, was a soldier, poet, and life-long member of the Scout movement, and is now best remembered as a former Supreme Magus of the S.R.I.A. whose name is perpetuated in that of the 'Michael Penrose College S.R.I.A.' in Chingford. Anyone seeking further information concerning his front-line experiences in Gallipoli during the 1st World War, or his achievements during a lifetime in scouting, is directed to the updated 'History of the S.R.I.A.' by T.M.Greensill, edited and re-printed by Andrew Stephenson in 1986. As far as the new Acon ritual is concerned, it was he who persuaded Walker to reduce to manageable proportions the historical account of the Order originally related by the Chapel Historian (i.e. Walker himself) but these days explained by four 'Working Knights'.

John Jary
Was a financial consultant, a Grand officer in most things, and an inveterate 'founder' and financial benefactor of small Orders (especially Knights Templar). It was he who produced the many revised versions of the ritual after Andrew Stephenson had re-typed them.

There were, of course, others who also played an active part in the early days of the Order and thereby helped to ensure its survival. For instance Howard Stokes (a former Grand Clerk of the Operatives, and the first Grand Master of the Pilgrim Preceptors); Benson F.Catt; Allan B. Perry, who managed its finances; Cyril Batham (a Past Master of Quatuor Coronati Lodge No. 2076, editor of its Transactions, and a former Prestonian Lecturer); Howard F. Doe; Keith Ansell; Gordon M.Gentry; and, of course, Barry Clarke

St. Thomas of Acon

who, when he became Grand Master in 1997, decided to open the Order to a wider membership, as will be explained.

At this point, it is hoped that it will be sufficient to conclude this chapter by recording that these were the members who, between them, refined from John Walker's researches, a workable modern ritual and a set of Statutes, to facilitate a 'chapel' of the Order meeting twice a year to commemorate the worthy sentiments of those Englishmen who had founded the original Order. Solely out of convenience, those meetings were invariably timed to coincide with the meetings of other Orders, Acon generally meeting in the morning, and one of the other small Orders meeting in the afternoon.

It might be of interest to note that, in its early days, most of the original members wore Knight Templar regalia to those meetings but, over the years, an increasing number began to acquire their own distinctive Acon regalia, similar to that of the original Order, wearing a variety of scallop shells on their tunics and in their hats, sometimes obtained - through the kind offices of Keith Ansell - from such unlikely sources as the beaches and fish-shops of East Anglia! Despite the low-key nature of its start, however, and the unlikely sources of some of their regalia, the enthusiasm of its members continued undiminished and, gradually, the outlines of a totally new commemorative masonic Order became discernible, ready for the next stage in its evolution.

CHAPTER 2

The Order expands

In November 1997 Andrew Stephenson who had succeeded John Walker as Grand Master six years earlier, passed the reins of office - with a minimum of formality - to Barry Clarke, whose election was confirmed by the Grand Master's Council on 13th December, 1997. Well known as an accomplished ritualist, for his facility with classical languages, and for his easy-going personality, he was a popular choice, especially since, by that time, he had been a member of the chapel for fifteen years and was totally familiar with its ritual and Statutes. He was a member of most Orders of English freemasonry and was a Grand Officer in all of them, including the Order of the Secret Monitor, of which he was the Provincial Grand Supreme Ruler for Essex, and the Societas Rosicruciana in Anglia, of which he was the Chief Adept for the Province of East Anglia (i.e. Essex, Suffolk, Cambridgeshire and Norfolk).

Equally well received was *his* early announcement that he was willing for membership of Acon to be increased beyond the limit previously necessitated by the size of the temple in Andrew Stephenson's house which, by then, had become cramped and dangerous because of the number (and weight!) of those crowding into the upstairs 'temple', which had never been designed for such loads.

The consequences of that decision were dramatic. By the end of 1997, having already been in existence for well over twenty years, there were still only twenty-five members of the Order, namely: Keith Ansell, Desmond Bourke, John Brackley, Michael Buckley, Ian Burnett, Benson Catt, Barry Clarke, Gerard Crane, Howard Doe, James Field, Gordon Gentry, David Kibble-Rees, Timothy Lewis, Brian Lobb, John Mannock, John Mitchell, Alan

St. Thomas of Acon

Monk, Brian Muir, Allan Perry, David Price, Thomas Purnell, Colin Spencer, Andrew Stephenson, Ian Tough, and Patrick Wilkins.

Within two years, however, membership had increased by seven hundred percent! Over two hundred candidates had been admitted in a series of extra-ordinary meetings (or 'cavalry charges' as they came to be known) and new chapels had been consecrated in Wickford, Chingford, Leyland, Dewsbury and Canterbury, with additional interest being expressed by freemasons elsewhere in England and Wales, and as far afield as France, Spain, Australia and North America.

In retrospect it is difficult to explain this enthusiasm. It might have been because its origins were known to be historically accurate (as distinct from 'allegorical', which is more usual in freemasonry), as explained in the ritual when every candidate for Acon is told: 'This Order is based on historical facts in every part thereof, as may be confirmed by you through an examination of various documents and records dating back to the 13th century held in the library of the City of London in Guildhall.' Alternatively, it might have been the Christian ideas of humility and compassion which provided so strong an appeal, or simply the fact that it was something new.

Whatever the reason, within six years, the Chapel at Blackheath had been transferred to Mark Masons' Hall in St. James's Street, London, and new Chapels had been established at:

<u>1998</u>
Wickford

<u>1999</u>
Chingford
Leyland
Dewsbury
Canterbury

<u>2000</u>
Carnforth
Macclesfield
Harrow
Chester
York
Pittsburgh (USA)
Washington DC (USA)
Birmingham

The Order expands

Chester-le-Street
Ontario (Canada)

2001
Great Yarmouth
Duffield
Rugeley
Middlesborough
Pontefract
Llanfairfechan
Eastbourne

2002
Redditch
Mansfield
Ormskirk
Clare

2003
Liskeard
Harlow
Burnley
Tacoma (USA)

The year 2003 has been chosen as the end of this particular period because, in November of that year the Grand Master found it necessary to submit his resignation, but it should never be forgotten that in only six years he had transformed the Order from one numerically-insignificant 'chapel', meeting in an upstairs room in a private house in Blackheath, into a nationally-recognised masonic Order with thirty 'chapels' and hundreds of members. The ritual had been refined to accommodate critics of the Eucharist and Agape; Statutes had been altered to 'Constitutions for the government of the Order', and increased in number to reflect its status as an independent Order; the list of officers had been amended (e.g. the role of the Chapel Historian had been transferred to four 'Working Knights'); decisions had been taken concerning the future design of Grand and Provincial banners and swords; the first three Provinces had been established, with 'Grand Preceptors' in charge; and a programme drawn up for the future development of the Order. It had

St. Thomas of Acon

been six years of frenetic activity during which the Order had become firmly established as a masonic entity.

On 29th December 2003 Rt. Rev. Bishop Gerard Crane, the Grand Prior, was appointed a 'Knight Humilitas', and John Wallace Mitchell and Keith Ansell were appointed 'Knights Caritas'. Two years later, when he felt able to resume his Masonic career, Barry Clarke was appointed a 'Knight Humilitas'. In all four cases this was in recognition of all they had done during an incredibly hectic period to ensure that the Order became firmly established as a constituent part of the Masonic community.

CHAPTER 3

Continued expansion

Following the surprise resignation of the Grand Master in 2003, but the necessary machinery of government having been put in place for such an eventuality, the Executive Committee (under the chairmanship of the Grand Prior, Rt. Rev'd Bishop Gerard J. Crane) then met and unanimously decided to recommend the appointment of David Kibble-Rees (the author of this book) as the fourth Grand Master. This was put to the Grand Master's Council and approved on 29th December 2003. As a former Grand Treasurer, he had been privy to the intricacies of policy-making within the Order up to that point and, because of that, the fact that he was already a Grand Preceptor, and his experience in other Orders and Societies, he was considered suitably qualified for the role.

The new Grand Master began his term of office with just four objectives in mind, which were :

To promote the image of the Order

This had become necessary because, although the Order had expanded, that expansion was more than some of its earlier members welcomed, in addition to which there were those who thought it might encroach upon the interests of other Orders. There were also a few outsiders who did everything they could to thwart further development, and some who even denied its right to exist!

Because of all those things, determined efforts were made to ensure its future masonic 'acceptability' and to reassure its detractors that they had nothing to fear from the Order which, in fact, had already existed for over a quarter of a century without troubling anyone. One critic, with no apparent justification , had actually gone so far so far as to describe Acon as a pariah amongst masonic Orders! Happily, such comments were rare and, in recent years,

St. Thomas of Acon

have ceased entirely. In fact, there are now enough senior officers of other Orders within the membership of Acon that it is safe to assume that such unjustifiable and unfraternal comments are things of the past.

Other innovations calculated to promote the image of the Order were the creation of a Website, the circulation of a Newsletter (the 'Acon Herald'), and ensuring that, wherever possible, the Order was referred to in the Year Books of other Orders.

To continue the programme of expansion

It will be recalled that when, in 1998, it was decided to open the Order to a wider membership, there was only one chapel but that, within the next six years, that number had risen to thirty-one. Well, that rate of expansion continued, and during the succeeding years new Chapels were established, as follows:

<u>2004</u>
Penarth
Port Talbot
Ashington
Alicante (Spain)
Melbourne (Australia)
Perth (Australia)
Widnes
Long Eaton

<u>2005</u>
Radlett
Carmarthen
Chepstow
Sydney (Australia)
Redhill
Bryan, Texas (USA)
Houston (USA)
Brisbane (Australia)
Dallas (USA)
Aukland (NZ)
West Bridgeford
Newmarket
New York (USA)

Continued expansion

2006
Fishguard
Monroe (USA)
San Antonio (USA)
Chichester
Columbia (USA)
Morgantown (USA)

2007
Wokingham
Tollesbury
Gloucester
Warwick
Fort Worth (USA)
Gillingham
London
Orlando (USA)
Mississauga (Canada)
Regina (Canada)
Ashby-de-la-Zouch
Melbourne (Australia)
Delaware (USA)

2008
Crediton
Watford
Bath

The Order's current membership is approximately 2000.

To enhance the status of the Annual Pilgrimage
It has already been explained that, in its early days, it had been decided that an Annual Pilgrimage would be a distinguishing characteristic of the Order, but that its first attempts in the 1970s amounted to little more than a few members making a collective visit to Canterbury Cathedral.
As the Order grew, however, it became apparent that something more was required, so an appropriate Service was devised and held in the Crypt of the Cathedral by Rt.Rev.Bishop

St. Thomas of Acon

Gerard Crane, the Grand Prior of the Order, and since continued by Michael Harridine, who is an ordained minister of the United Reformed Church as well as the Grand Preceptor of the Province of London and the South Eastern Counties. Its popularity has grown year upon year, and members of the Order from as far as Australia, the USA and Canada are now frequent attenders. The Pilgrimage is open to all members, their friends and their families, and those members of the Order who have attended are entitled to wear a small representation of Becket's coat-of-arms on their regalia, to commemorate their attendance. In 2007 the total attendance was one-hundred-and-sixty.

The Order regularly makes donations to the upkeep of Canterbury Cathedral, which is its only official charity.

To relocate the meetings of the Grand Master's Council

Because, during the time of its first Grand Master, it had been decided that ultimate authority would be vested in the Grand Master's Council, and that meetings would be organised along the lines of those of any other Grand Lodge, it soon became apparent that a suitable venue would have to be found to accommodate the representatives of the ever-increasing number of Chapels and Provinces. When the Order consisted of only one Chapel that had presented no difficulty and, if necessary, they could have met in a telephone box! By 2003, however, things were very different. In 1998, for example, the attendance had only been 9; in 1999 it had been 19; and in 2000 it had been 17. By 2003 attendance had doubled and was giving every sign of increasing still further, commensurate with the increased number of Chapels.

The new Grand Master therefore decided to relocate meetings from the Thistle Hotel in Bloomsbury, London, to the Masonic Hall in Littleover, Derby, which was conveniently located in the centre of the country, easy to reach for the members of most Chapels, and equidistant for those with furthest to travel in this country, namely Ashington (Durham), Canterbury (Kent) and Liskeard (Cornwall). The results were immediate and attendances in the following four years were:

2004	63 attended
2005	77
2006	87
2007	104

Continued expansion

Those figures speak for themselves, and the Grand Master's Council is now firmly established in Littleover. It meets on 29th December annually, which is the Feast Day of St. Thomas and the anniversary of his Martyrdom.

The end of this second period, therefore, saw the Order more than doubled in size, acceptable to other masonic Orders, unique in being the only Order with an official Pilgrimage, and with its most important meeting (i.e. the Grand Master's Council) taking place on 29th December annually in Derbyshire.

Although he would like to mention everyone who has contributed to the development of the Order, especially over the last ten years, it would be impractical to attempt to do so. But it would be remiss if this chapter were to be concluded without the author making special reference to three of its members, each of whom daily demonstrates a degree of commitment far in excess of that usually described as 'above and beyond the call of duty', and has thereby helped to bring Acon to the healthy state that it is in today. They are John Loat, Andre Lovas and Kent Henderson. John Loat has been the Grand Secretary since 2003 and seemingly spends every waking moment of every single day, administering the Order from a room in his house. Eventually this will obviously have to come to an end but, until it does, only those who have regular dealings with him will know the full extent of his commitment and how much the Order owes to him. He was appointed a 'Knight Caritas' in 2005. Andre Lovas is the Grand Preceptor for the 'Province of the United States of America', which is easy to say but not quite so easy to administer, and involves giving up vast amounts of time and travelling huge distances. The USA, it must be remembered, consists of fifty States and one Federal District, so his duties entail not merely visiting the Chapels in his Province but liaising with numerous Grand Lodges and attending many other Orders, if only to 'wave the flag' for Acon. Kent Henderson is also a Grand Preceptor and similarly has to deal with the freemasons in a number of different States, and his Province is that of 'Australia and New Zealand' which, geographically, is probably as big as that of the USA, and necessitates his going through Time Zones as frequently as most of us go through traffic-lights! In that connection, a few years back, the author was present when the two of them were jokingly discussing the question of who was responsible for the biggest Province of the Order. Andre Lovas asserted he was, pointing out that, in addition to

St. Thomas of Acon

mainland USA, there were also the American States of Hawaii and Alaska to be considered, to which Kent Henderson responded by reminding everyone that he was responsible not just for Australia (including the Capital and Northern Territories) but also for Tasmania and New Zealand. The discussion came to an end when Andre Lovas claimed the Moon as part of his Province, American astronauts having established a presence by planting masonic artifacts there during one of their missions! It was a happy occasion and a friendly discussion but one it is impossible to forget when anyone mentions the word 'commitment' in connection with freemasonry. There are many to whom the Order should be grateful, but these three - in particular – consistently 'go the extra mile'!

CHAPTER 4

The Order today

The Commemorative Masonic Order of St. Thomas of Acon today is a totally independent and fully established member of the masonic community in England, Wales, Spain, the USA, Canada, Australia and New Zealand. It has over two thousand members meeting in seventy-eight 'Chapels', most of which have been grouped into Provinces, of which there are currently ten. Membership can only be obtained 'by invitation' and is limited to freemasons who are already subscribing members of a Knights Templar Preceptory.

Its most senior member is its Grand Master, who is assisted by a Grand Prior and a number of other Grand Officers whose duties correspond with those of the Grand officers of virtually all other masonic Orders. Provinces are administered by Grand Preceptors, assisted by their own Provincial officers, the titles and duties of whom correspond with those of Grand officers.

The officers assisting the Grand Master, a Grand Preceptor, or the Worthy Master of a Chapel are:

Prior
Marshal
Treasurer
Registrar*
Secretary
Historian*
Deputy Marshal
Almoner
Sword Bearer
Deputy Secretary*
Banner Bearer
Assistant Marshal*

St. Thomas of Acon

Assistant Secretary*
Herald
Organist
Doorkeeper
Cellarer(s)
Sentry

* indicates officers only appointed at Grand or Provincial level

Most Chapels meet twice a year, but the Grand officers (together with the Masters and Priors of all the Chapels) meet in the Grand Masters' Council, on 29th December of each year, that being the Feast Day of St. Thomas a Becket, after whom the Order is named. Grand Preceptors similarly preside over the annual Provincial Grand Councils in their various Provinces.

The Order is governed by 'The Grand Master's Council'.

The Banner of the Order depicts the Arms of the Order and comprises: argent (34") a cross rouge (4.5" in width) reaching to the edge of the banner, on which is superimposed a white cross (1.5" in width, terminating 1.5" from the edges of the banner). The Banner is charged with a gold Escallope shell (fimbriated rouge) edged in the first quarter. It is borne on a carrying pole (i.e. Not suspended from a cross bar). The banners of Provinces are similar to that of the Grand Master but are charged with an additional device representing the Jurisdiction Territory in the second quarter. Where appropriate this device must be fimbriated. Private Chapels use a banner similar to that of their Province charged with an additional device representing their Chapel placed centrally at the intersection of the arms of the Cross.

Knights of the Order wear a tunic of stone-white material, long enough to cover the knees, fastened at the back. On the front is a Latin Cross four inches wide, the full length of the tunic, colour Medici Crimson, on which is superimposed a white Latin Cross one third of the width. The centre of the intersection of the Cross is charged with an Escallope shell (coloured bronze for Knights, silver for Provincial officers, gold for Grand officers). Over the tunic, Knights wear a mantle, of similar stone-white material to the tunic with a hood of the same material lined with white silk. On the left shoulder of the mantle there is a Greek Cross (straight limbs of ten inches in length) divided vertically and horizontally red, white, red in even widths of 0.5 inches, the white cross terminating 0.5 inches short of the ends of the cross. The midpoint of the Cross is charged with an Escallope shell,

The Order today

similar to, but smaller than, that worn on the tunic. Knights also wear a crimson velvet cap, three inches deep; on the front of the cap there is a single Escallope shell, smaller than that on the mantle. The shell is always worn upright (i.e. with the hinge of the shell at the bottom and fan opening at the top).

In their Chapels, Masters of Chapels carry a Sceptre, on the top of which is a large bronze Escallope shell. Grand Preceptors carry a Sceptre bearing a Silver shell, and the Grand Master carries a Sceptre bearing a Gold shell. All Knights (apart from Priors and Almoners) wear a sword and scabbard suspended from a leather belt, two inches in width.

The highest honours which may be conferred by the Grand Master, at his discretion, are:
Knight Humilitas (maximum number 10) of which there are currently three.
Knight Caritas (maximum number 15) of which there are currently five.
In both cases the Knight concerned wears a collarette bearing the letters 'KC' or KH' (as appropriate).

The Order periodically publishes a newsletter, "The Acon Herald", and has a website which can be found at www.orderofstthomasofacon.org

The Order is unique in that its members are enjoined to make at least one official Pilgrimage to Canterbury Cathedral at some time during their membership of the Order. Pilgrimages take place in late November of each year, the precise date depending on the Cathedral's commitments, and those who have made such a Pilgrimage are entitled to wear an appropriate badge commemorating that fact on the right shoulder of their mantles. Canterbury Cathedral is the Order's only official Charity.

CHAPTER 5

St. Thomas à Becket

In this chapter it is not proposed to burden the reader by repeating just another account of Becket's meteoric rise to the high offices of Chancellor and Archbishop; or his early friendship and subsequent conflict with King Henry II over the Constitutions of Clarendon; or even his murder in Canterbury Cathedral. Enough has been written about all those things already. Indeed, it has been said that more has been written about Becket than almost anyone else in history! Therefore, bearing in mind that he was dead, buried and canonised before this Order came into existence, it is proposed to utilise this opportunity by clarifying four points, none of which is essential to an understanding of him as a man but, collectively, are important to an appreciation of his role as far as the Order is concerned. They are:

The uncertainty surrounding his name;
The persistent legend surrounding his mother;
His popularity as a martyr; and
Why the 12th Century founders of a new Order chose to name it after him.

Uncertainty surrounding his name
Thomas Becket was born in or around 1118 CE in Ironmonger Lane, Cheapside which, at the time, was just one of a conglomeration of small, heavily populated wards and parishes which collectively made up the City of London and which, since earliest times, has been referred to as 'the square mile'. His parents were Gilbert and Matilda Becket, whose families originated in Normandy

but came to England following the Norman invasion. Originally there was no 'à' to his name, and that only seems to have been added later, possibly to lend it a degree of resonance (and maybe importance) or even link it in some way to that of Thomas à Kempis, the 14th century monk and author of the 'Imitation of Christ'. His father was a mercer and Port Reeve (i.e. chief officer) of the City of London, whose family came from Thierceville. They were fairly affluent (i.e. burgesses, or upper middle class) and they had at least three other children, Mary, Roessa and Agnes. Eventually, both parents were buried in the Pardon Churchyard of the St. Paul's Cathedral which was destroyed in the Great Fire of London, either because – according to John Stow's 'Survey of London' – Gilbert Becket is said to have financed the building of a chapel there or, more likely, because their local church (St. Mary Colechurch in Cheapside) was one of those without burial facilities.

The legend surrounding his mother

Despite strong evidence to support the view that his mother came from Caen, there is an enduring legend that, when young, Gilbert (i.e. Thomas's father) joined a crusade and, at some point, was captured by a Moor who imprisoned him. With the assistance of the Moor's daughter, who had apparently fallen in love with him, he eventually escaped and made his way back to London to where, in due course, she followed him, despite the fact that she knew no English, apart from the words 'Gilbert' and 'London'. According to the legend, she was then baptised into the Christian faith, they were married, and - as is usual with romantic tales - they lived happily ever after! It is only fair to add that, nowadays, this legend is treated with scepticism, although it also has to be acknowledged that there are nevertheless those historians who rigidly adhere to its reliability. Prior to their destruction, the legend was illustrated in the stained-glass windows of the Mercer's Company church in Ironmonger Lane; it is frequently referred to in books (e.g. Robert Lomas's *'The Secrets of Freemasonry'*, 2006, and Augustus J.C.Hare's book *'Walks in London'* Vol.1,1878) and on the Internet (e.g. in Chapter 1 of *'The Golden Falcon'*, which is an on-line biography of the Winter family), and the author of this book has heard it referred to during the course of one of the guided 'London Walks' popular with visitors to the capital. Suffice it to say that some believe it whilst others do not. As far as this Order is concerned, Walker was one of those who

St. Thomas à Becket

accepted it, which is how and why he came to include it in the ritual of the revived Order.

Becket's popularity

Although never particularly popular during his lifetime, especially within certain sections of the Church, the reaction to Becket's murder, and the devotion accorded to him thereafter, was nothing less than amazing. Hence the reason the Pope promulgated a bull of canonisation less than three years after his death, and King Henry's display of penance in 1174, when he was publicly scourged on his way to the archbishop's tomb, even though he had been absolved from guilt by the Pope two years earlier. According to the Catholic Encyclopedia, Becket's tomb eventually became 'one of the wealthiest and most famous in Europe', and churches, schools and hospitals throughout the country were dedicated to his memory, such as St. Thomas's Hospital in Southwark; St. Thomas's Hospital, Sandwich; the Hospital of St. Thomas the Martyr at Canterbury, which has been fully restored and opened to the public, and provides an authentic representation of the facilities provided for pilgrims in the 13th century; and the still-standing Hospital Chapel of St. Mary the Virgin and St. Thomas the Martyr of Canterbury in Ilford, the name of which was increased to include that of Becket as the result of a request from Henry II to Mary, Becket's sister, who was the Abbess of Barking Abbey, and responsible for that hospital, which was intended to accommodate thirteen Brethren. Other examples are the church of St. Thomas on the new London Bridge opened in 1205; the 'Chantry Chapel and Royal Latin School' in Buckingham, which is the oldest building in Buckingham and, 'since time immemorial', is known to have been dedicated to St. Thomas of Acon; and, of course, the Hospital and Church of St. Thomas opened by Agnes, another of Becket's sisters, in Cheapside, London. There were countless others.

The reason the original Order was named after Becket

Given the preceding paragraph, one might reasonably be excused for thinking that his popularity alone was enough for an Order to be named after him during the course of the 3rd Crusade, but such a conclusion would be insufficient and take no account of the personal connection between Becket and at least three other clerics who were arguably even more important to the foundation of the

St. Thomas of Acon

Order than him, namely Ralph de Diceto, 'William the Englishman', and Baldwin of Exeter.

Ralph de Diceto was appointed Dean of St. Paul's in 1180 CE and is known to have been highly respected for his learning and integrity as well as for having built a deanery at his own expense. He was more than just that, however, and is now best remembered as the author of three major chronicles of his time, the 'Abbreviationes Chronicorum', 'Ymagines Historiarum' (which contains an account of the Order's origins), and a 'Domesday' record of the estates of St.Paul's. He was, in fact, a contemporary of Becket and is known to have shown a certain amount of sympathy for his views at the council of Northampton in 1164. What is more, he is known to have dedicated one of St. Paul's west gallery altars to the martyr who, at one time, had been one of his fellow-canons at St. Paul's, so it would seem that he not only knew him but, so far as was possible at that time, respected him.

The man now known only as 'William the Englishman' is just as important to an understanding of Becket as Diceto, because he was Diceto's chaplain. Moreover, he is known to have been 'architecturally-inclined'; to have been responsible for completing the choir at Canterbury Cathedral between 1177 and 1184 after its original architect (William of Sens) was injured in a fall; and is thought to have been responsible for the west front and vaults of St. Paul's in London. He was therefore in an ideal position for knowing Diceto's feelings, and for acquiring an appreciation of the extent of the public's affection for the murdered Saint. More significantly, he was the same 'William the Englishman' who, during his journey to Acre at the start of the 3rd Crusade, vowed that if he reached and entered that city, he would build there a Chapel to St. Thomas the Martyr at his own expense, and thereafter devote himself to burying the dead, all of which he did.

The third of these clerics, Baldwin of Exeter, was Archbishop of Canterbury from 1185 until 1190 and led a force of five thousand to take part in the Siege of Acre during the 3rd Crusade, under a banner inscribed with the name 'Thomas à Becket'. Although the sight of such a force would have been welcomed by those besieging Acre, and no doubt gave heart to the English amongst them, there are those who have always doubted if it actually did anything for Christianity. Although undoubtedly brave, distinguished and religious, Baldwin has since been described as 'injudicious and too austere to be a good leader' and, strangely, as 'a greater enemy of

St. Thomas à Becket

Christianity than Saladin'! Fortunately, in this chapter, we are considering Becket and not Baldwin so, notwithstanding those reservations, it seems not unreasonable to assume that the presence in Acre of a large English force under a banner inscribed with the Saint's name, is likely to have had at least some impact on anyone thinking about finding a suitable name for a new Order.

It is not proposed to labour these points any further. The fact is that there were many reasons for naming a new Order after Becket. He was universally revered as a Saint and, in retrospect, the surprising thing would have been if it had been named after anyone else!

All of which also explains why it was that the Founders of the Commemorative Masonic Order ensured that, at the meal which follows every meeting of the Order, and before any formal Toasts are taken, its members always observe 'The Commemoration' and drink 'To the pious memory of St. Thomas à Becket and the glorious memory of the Knights of the Order who fought in the Crusades'.

CHAPTER 6

The Crusades

In this chapter, it is not intended to attempt a summary of all the Crusades which have occurred during the past thousand years, some of which involved territories far removed from the Holy Land and were not necessarily directed against Islam. Instead it is proposed to concentrate on the 1st and 2nd Crusades, simply to set the scene, and the 3rd Crusade, because it was then that the Order of St. Thomas of Acon was founded. Nor is it intended to enter into any form of judgment as to whether they were a good or a bad thing, whether they were heroic, or whether anyone should now be ashamed of the conduct of some of those who took part. Suffice it to say that they took place, and they were the birthplace of many of the military Orders which flourished in the Middle Ages. Being concerned with the history of an Order, as distinct from an analysis of the Crusades, the only comment that is necessary here is that, over the years, opinions have differed widely regarding their legacy, and have always been influenced by the times and perspective of those making the assessment.

Preamble to the 1st Crusade

In March 1095 the Emperor of Byzantium, sent ambassadors to Pope Urban II at the Council of Piacenza asking for support against the Seljuk Turks who were threatening his Empire. Whether the immediacy of the threat was his sole reason for doing so is not known. Whatever the reason, ambassadors were sent and an appeal for support was received.

Just as we cannot be sure of the reason for his appeal, so we cannot now be certain as to why the Pope responded as strongly as he did. It is known, for instance that, like the Emperor, he, too, had his problems at that time, mostly arising from his support for the

St. Thomas of Acon

reforms of Pope Gregory VII, and the rival claims of the so-called anti-Pope, Clement III. It might equally have been because he saw a Holy War as a 'good cause'. Whatever his reason, on 27th November 1095 the Pope relayed that appeal to the Council of Clermont, where he was supported by Adhemar of Monteil (the Bishop of Le Puy) and, as of that moment, a crusade against the Muslims in the Holy Land was a certainty, although it wasn't referred to as such at the time, the word 'crusade' (from the French 'croisade') only being adopted many years later, from the distinctive crosses worn by those taking part. He spent most of the following year touring Italy and France, mainly promoting his own popularity but, at the same time, gathering support for a 'Holy War', the objectives of which were: To defend the Christians in Byzantium; to protect the Holy Sepulchre and other places which were being defiled; and to preserve the rights of pilgrims which were being challenged.

Before describing the Crusades, however, it is proposed to digress, in order to describe those who took part and their motivation for going.

The first Crusaders

It has previously been mentioned that, although a number of other nations were involved, the first crusaders were predominantly French, a natural consequence of which was that the movement as a whole was never referred to as being composed of crusaders, pilgrims, Germans or Italians, but of 'Franks'. This was hardly surprising, given the origins of the Pope (who came from Largery, near Chatillon-sur-Marne) and his strongest supporter, the Bishop of Le Puy, (whose diocese was about 140 km south-west of Lyon). In fact the majority of those who took part were drawn from regions we now regard as France, which explains why the Bishop of Le Puy was appointed Papal Legate to the first of the Crusades and Count Raymond IV of Toulouse was nominated its military leader.

It seems that the Pope's original plan was for a representative number of the more noble families of France (of which he was himself a member) to assemble during the summer of 1096 and, about the middle of August, begin making their orderly way in 'waves' to Byzantium, where they were to assemble near Constantinople, before proceeding on to Jerusalem. It was estimated that it would take that amount of time for those involved to raise whatever funds were necessary, to get their arms, equipment and armies together, and make arrangements for the families and estates left behind whilst they were away.

As is usual with the best laid plans, however, things soon went awry and the first to set out were not the noble families he'd hoped for, but 'Peter the Hermit' (a monk from Amiens) and Walter Sans-Avoir ('Walter the Penniless'), an impoverished knight who, having few possessions or responsibilities, found it easy to jump the gun and set out before anyone else at the head of an ill-equipped rabble of unarmed men, women and children, and make their way towards the Holy Land, murdering, robbing and pillaging as they went. It seems unnecessary to add that these were nothing like the noble-warriors the Pope had in mind as the saviors of Christendom but, having called on anyone and everyone to make the pilgrimage, as a sort of devotional duty, when they responded in their thousands he was powerless to stop them. Subsequent 'waves' included more responsible members of society, such as merchants, craftsmen and farmers and, during the course of that Summer, they were followed by knights and, finally, by the Bishop of Le Puy and Count Raymond of Toulouse.

Why did anyone go on Crusade?

Although the reasons for going on crusade varied over time, those making the 1st Crusade did so for two main reasons, which may be summarized as 'spiritual' and 'temporal'.

The spiritual reasons centered around the power and authority of the Church. It must be remembered that, in the 11th century, apart from the clergy, hardly anyone was able to read and write, let alone understand Latin, so the authority of the church was total. Consequently, few knew the geographical whereabouts of Jerusalem, although everyone knew of its importance and, as a result, when a call was made by the Church to go on crusade, they simply took it as a sort of 'command from on high' and went. And in case it should be felt that such a suggestion is to trivialise the Pope's exhortation, it should be remembered that the insistent rallying cry of the 1st Crusade, whether at meetings beforehand or during the long and arduous march, was 'Deus lo vault', meaning 'God wills it', in addition to which the Pope had given the compelling promise that 'All who die by the way, whether by land or by sea, or in battle against the pagans, shall have immediate remission of sins'.

St. Thomas of Acon

That was not, of course, the sole extent of the influence exerted by the Church, representatives of which were known to stage-manage public meetings in order to gain support, and to offer 'indulgences' to those willing to go, such as a release from excommunication, or the right to have a personal confessor, with wide powers of absolution from their sins. It also gave the reassuring promise that it would protect their families and estates whilst they were away. All of which were linked to two impressive ceremonies, one dramatically involving 'taking the cross' and a second involving being formally presented with the symbols of pilgrimage, i.e. a scrip purse and staff, which they were enjoined to carry until they had fulfilled their vow, the emotional impact of which was described by Sir Walter Raleigh many years later, when he wrote:

> "Give me my scallop-shell of quiet,
> My staff of faith to walk upon,
> My scrip of joy, immortal diet,
> My bottle of salvation,
> My gown of glory, hope's true gage;
> And thus I'll take my pilgrimage."

Temporal reasons were equally persuasive, and included: A delay in the performance of feudal services or in judicial proceedings until their return; a moratorium on the repayment of debt; and an exemption from all tithes and taxes. And linked to those, of course, were those rewards soldiers have always found most difficult to resist, which were the lure of adventure and the possibility of acquiring fame and fortune, all of which were even more compelling at a time when the Law of Primogeniture prevailed. For the second and subsequent sons of titled families considering going on crusade, such a venture held out the tempting promise of a solution to what was probably the most pressing of their problems.

In all fairness it has to be said that, for many years, greed, adventure, and the lure of fame and fortune, were regarded as the sole motivation of all those going on crusade. In recent years, however, it has been realised that this has been to simplify their reasons for going which, for many, were genuinely more akin to an errand of mercy, or the ultimate pilgrimage, either of which they were willing to perform for the most sincere of reasons. The truth, it would

The Crusades

seem, is that the first crusaders were probably motivated by a complex mix of all these reasons, and the important thing is not to assume they were simply one or the other.

The 1st Crusade (1095-1099)

These, then, were the people who took part in the 1st Crusade and some of their reasons for going. As explained, those with Peter the Hermit and Walter the Penniless were the first to leave, travelling overland through Germany and Hungary (as they are now known), and the last were Count Raymond of Toulouse and Bishop Adhemar of Monteil, who travelled by way of southern Italy, across the Adriatic, and through Greece. Between them came various 'waves', using a variety of routes, all destined to assemble in Constantinople, including: Duke Godfrey of Bouillon, accompanied by his brothers Eustace and Baldwin and an army of 40, 000; Count Bohemond of Taranto (a small kingdom in southern Italy) accompanied by his nephew, Tancred of Hautville; and Duke Robert of Normandy (the son-in-law of William the Conqueror), accompanied by Count Stephen of Blois and Count Robert of Flanders.

As might be expected, the Peasants' Crusade led by Peter the Hermit arrived in July 1096 but, being nothing like the noble band of warriors the Emperor expected when he first made his appeal for support, he lost no time in ferrying them across the Bosporous and speeding them on their way to Jerusalem. Not surprisingly they were ambushed on their way and virtually wiped out. Those who survived either gave up and went home, or returned to Constantinople to join up with the main group. By the Spring of 1097 the Crusade-proper was ready for its Holy War and began the last leg of its journey to Jerusalem. En route they were engaged in a number of sieges and battles, the most important of which were the Siege of Nicaea, which lasted from 14th May until 19th June 1097; the Battle of Dorylaeum, which took place on 1st July 1097; the Siege of Antioch, which lasted for about nine months and ended on 3rd June 1098; and the unusual but bloodless 'acquisition' of Edessa by Baldwin and a small force of knights, whereby Edessa became the first of the 'Crusader States'.

On 7th June 1099, the main body of the Crusade finally arrived outside Jerusalem and began a siege which ended on 15th July, on which date they entered the city, killing virtually anyone and everyone who stood in their way. In the words of William of Malmesbury: "Such a slaughter of pagans no one has ever seen or heard of. The pyres (of bodies) they made were like pyramids". Eight days later the Christian Kingdom of Jerusalem was proclaimed, with Godfrey of Bouillon as its head, thereby bringing the first of the Crusades to an end.

Pope Urban, who had called for the Crusade four years earlier, died one week later, never knowing the outcome of the Holy War he had started.

The 2nd Crusade (1145-1149)

It would be understandable if one felt a degree of 'déjà vu' when first encountering the 2nd Crusade in as much as, like the 1st Crusade, the initial call came from a Pope in response to a request from the East, arising from the aggression of Seljuk Turks, and was preached at emotionally charged meetings, by a cleric renowned for his oratory. The indulgences proffered were identical to those extended to the 1st Crusade and, as before, the church once again guaranteed the safety of wives, families and property left behind by those 'taking the cross'. As with the 1st Crusade, it was planned to devote a year to making preparations before going overland to Constantinople. Further similarities included both Crusades attacking Jewish communities wherever and whenever they encountered them, and, in both cases, being totally antipathetic towards their hosts in Byzantium. With that, however, all similarity ended. Unlike the 1st Crusade, the 2nd was led by Kings, not nobles; there was little enthusiasm from *anyone* at the start, especially the nobility; a number of other nations took part, including the English, Scottish, Flemish and Provencals; it was never directed against a single enemy (one-third being directed against the Moors in Iberia, and the other third being directed against the Wends in northern Europe); and those crusading in the Holy Land never succeeded in capturing either their first or secondary objectives. If, therefore, one were to compare the two crusades, the 1st resulted in the capture of Jerusalem and the creation of four Crusader States, whereas the 2nd failed in every respect. (Author's note: That portion of the crusade directed against the Wends in northern Europe proved just as unsuccessful as that in the Holy Land, whilst those crusading in Iberia considered their duty done with the capture of Lisbon and either settled there or went home, although a few *did* continue by sea to Jerusalem.)

To put a little more flesh on the bones of this account, the event which provoked the 2nd Crusade was the re-capture by Seljuk Turks of Edessa which, as will be recalled, had been the first of the

The Crusades

States captured during the 1st Crusade but was also the least populated and the most vulnerable. The city itself has a history going back further than Alexander the Great and may even have been the site of Ur, the birthplace of Abraham. Whether ancient or not, in 1144 its ruler decided to leave it open and defenceless and rode out with his army in support of his one and only ally, Kara Aslan, the ruler of Diyarbakir. Unsurprisingly, it was promptly re-captured by the Turks, news of which was conveyed to Pope Eugenius III, who promptly issued a Bull calling for a 2nd Crusade to re-dress that loss.

The Bull was actually directed at King Conrad III of Germany (who was not really interested) and King Louis VII of France (who was planning to go on pilgrimage anyway, although not on crusade). In both cases, the factors which convinced them otherwise and eventually to 'take the Cross' were the fervour and oratory of Bishop Bernard of Clairvaux who (at Speyer) delivered a sermon which convinced Conrad, and (at Vezelay) had the same effect on Louis. The Germans left in May 1147 and the French one month later, both having agreed to meet in Constantinople.

In the event, Conrad arrived first but decided not to wait and proceeded on to Iconium, dividing his army in two, one half of which was promptly destroyed at Dorylaeum and the other half of which (led by Otto of Freising) marched towards the coast where it was also defeated, at Laodicea. Conrad himself was injured during the first of those engagements and, for a time, was compelled to return to Constantinople to recuperate.

Eventually the remnants of Conrad's army met up again with that of Louis and together they made their way south, ultimately reaching Antioch on 19th March 1148. By then, little was left of either army, those who had not been killed in battle having died of sickness. Eventually they reached Jerusalem, where they were re-joined by Conrad himself (whose health had been restored), Otto of Freising and what was left of the army defeated at Laodicea, and by the few who had travelled by sea from Lisbon. The stage was thus set for the final act of the drama which had been devised by the Pope and Bernard of Clairvaux four years earlier. What followed was more of a farce than a drama.

There apparently being uncertainty as to what to do or where to go once they reached Jerusalem, it was decided to call a meeting of the Haute Cour (the highest council in Jerusalem) to decide on a target for their crusading zeal. This was held at Acre on 24th June

St. Thomas of Acon

1148 and attended by all those mentioned, together with King Baldwin III of Jerusalem, his mother (and regent) Queen Melisende, the Grand Masters of the military Orders, and a variety of other clerical and secular leaders who, between them, unaccountably resolved not, as might be expected, to attempt to re-capture Edessa, the loss of which had provoked the crusade, but to attack Damascus, the ruler of which had shown consistent animosity towards the Seljuks who had captured Edessa, and was therefore more of an ally than an enemy.

The Siege of Damascus lasted for one week and failed for a number of reasons, including such trivial issues as who, amongst them, was to formally 'receive' the city when the siege came to an end. Unsurprisingly, they soon abandoned the idea entirely, and Conrad returned to Constantinople, whilst Louis resorted to being 'on pilgrimage' as distinct from 'on crusade' and decided to remain in Jerusalem over the Christmas and Easter periods, thereby bringing the 2nd Crusade to an uninspiring and overdue end.

The 3rd Crusade (1189-1192)

Four factors combined to make a third Crusade a certainty, which were: The vulnerability and disarray of the Crusader States revealed by the 2nd Crusade; the emergence of a charismatic Muslim leader, in the person of Salah ad-Din Yusuf ibn Ayyub (usually known as 'Saladin') capable of exploiting that vulnerability; the resounding defeat of the Crusader armies at the Battle of Hattin; and, finally, the loss of Jerusalem only a few weeks later. Of these, one in particular requires further explanation, and that is the reputation of Saladin.

Saladin was the Kurdish leader of both Syria and Egypt and the first to combine those two nations into a united military force. He was born in 1137 in Tikrit (in modern Iraq) and died on 4th March 1193 at Damascus where, centuries later, Kaiser Wilhelm II of Germany deposited a wreath on his tomb bearing the inscription 'To a Knight without fear or blame, who often had to teach his opponents the right way to practice chivalry'. It is unnecessary to outline his life and career in detail because his reputation is as bright today as it ever was. He was simply one of those great leaders in history for whom a single name was, and still is, enough. It was, for example, his ensign which was adopted by the leaders of the Egyptian Revolution as their flag in 1952 and, more recently, by the rulers of Palestine, Yemen and Iraq. Saddam Hussein, the deposed President of Iraq who, like Saladin, was a Sunni Muslim and born at

The Crusades

Tikrit, is said to have deliberately adopted 1937 as his 'official' birth date, so as to correspond with the 800th anniversary of that of Saladin and, during his time in power, did all he could to be regarded as a 'second Saladin'. And just as significant is the strange fact that the British army has for years used a reliable armoured-vehicle known as a 'Saladin'. In all accounts of the period, whether novels, films or historical records, he is invariably portrayed as a cultured, intelligent and determined leader, as highly respected by his enemies as his own army, and capable of great chivalry and kindness, of which countless examples have been recorded. He was, in short, one of the truly great leaders known to history.

To resume the account of the 3rd Crusade, the scale of the defeat of the Christian armies by Saladin at the Horns of Hattin in July 1187, followed by his capture of Jerusalem soon after, came as a total shock to the West. So much so that news of it was said to have caused the death of the Pope from 'shock'. Whether true or not is immaterial. The important thing is that it fell to his successor (Pope Gregory VIII) to issue the Bull *Audita tremendi* calling for a 3rd Crusade to redress that loss, although he did not live long enough to see it.

Once again the call for a Crusade was answered by Kings, this time by the three most powerful kings in Europe, namely Frederick I of Germany, Philip II of France, and Richard I of England. Frederick and his army used the overland route favoured by the 1st Crusade to get to the Holy Land, whilst Philip and Richard started out together, but parted at Lyon. Their two armies then came together again in Sicily, where they remained for the winter, before proceeding on to the Holy Land by sea.

It should not be assumed from this simple account that their journeys were without incident. For example, whilst en route Frederick led his army (estimated at 100,000) in two battles against the Seljuk Turks, at Philomelion and Iconium but, somewhat strangely, drowned whilst crossing a shallow river on 10th June 1190, following which most of his army gave up and went home, leaving only a remnant to continue the crusade. Richard occupied his time in Sicily to rectify a wrong suffered by his sister (Queen Joan) who had been imprisoned and deprived of her inheritance following the death of her husband, and used the opportunity to compel the new King of Sicily (by the simple expedient of looting and burning Messina) into signing a peace treaty, with himself, Richard and

St. Thomas of Acon

Philip as co-signatories. Philip then left Sicily and set sail for the Holy Land, whilst Richard followed soon after, making deviations, because of adverse weather, via Crete and Rhodes, to conquer Cyprus, which he achieved within sixteen days, mainly because of the unpopularity of its ruler, Isaac Komnenos. Eventually, Richard (with 4,000 men-at-arms and 4,000 foot soldiers), Philip (with an army of 10,000), and the remaining 1,000 of Frederick's army (now under the command of the Duke of Swabia) all met up again to take part in one of the most terrible sieges known to history. This took place at an ancient port which, over the centuries, has been variously known as Acre, Saint-Jean de Acre, Akko or Acon (the Anglicised version of the name) but, because it was the place from which both the original Order and the Commemorative Masonic Order of St. Thomas took their name, it is proposed to digress again in order to explain something of its history and why it was important.

Acre (or Akko) is today a moderately sized industrial city with a population of about 48,000. It is situated on the northern Mediterranean coast of Israel, about forty miles west of Galilee and fifteen miles north of Haifa, and has a history which can be traced for over five thousand years. Because it is bounded on three sides by the sea, and on the fourth by extensive fortifications, it has always been virtually impregnable. Joshua was unable to capture it in 1300 BC, and nor could either the biblical tribe of Asher, the Hasmoneans, or even Napoleon – who besieged the town for sixty-one days - in the nineteenth century. In the past, because of its value as a deep-water port, and its position on the east-west trade route, it was visited by Julius Caesar and Marco Polo, and so important did it eventually become that, by about 1180, it had supplanted Alexandria as the principal trading-centre for the eastern Mediterranean and by the mid-13th century was said to produce an annual revenue in excess of that of England. This continued thereafter, because of its easy accessibility for the Italian mercantile States, and possibly because it was the first place that economic and religious migrants encountered when travelling to the Holy Land. All of which hopefully explains why Napoleon, before retreating, is quoted as having said: 'Had Akko been mine, the world would have been mine'. Saladin obviously had equally strong views for, in 1187, following his capture of Jerusalem, he lost no time whatsoever in extending his conquest to include Tiberias, Ascalon and, of course, Acre.

To continue the account of the 3rd Crusade, following the fall of Jerusalem in October 1187, Guy of Lusignan, King of Jerusalem,

The Crusades

having failed to enlist the support of Conrad of Montferrat, and breaking a promise he had made earlier to Saladin, decided to recapture Acre with the intention of making it his new capital. He therefore took advantage of the temporary absence of Saladin, who was away in Syria, and marched on Acre, accompanied by an army of about 9,000 and a small force of knights from Sicily and Pisa and, on 28th August 1189, began besieging the city in which there was an army twice as big as his. His force was soon reinforced, however, by Danish, Flemish, French and English crusaders, including an army of 10,000 under Henry of Champagne, and a force of 5,000 from England, under Baldwin, the Archbishop of Canterbury, all of which provoked Saladin into returning from Syria (accompanied by Muslim volunteers from two continents) and joining the fray, which thereby placed him in the unusual position of besieging the besiegers. Acre at this stage, was therefore temporarily secure but under siege from Guy, whilst Guy and his army were themselves under siege and being attacked from behind. A sort of stalemate existed, which continued until the arrival of Philip on 20th April, 1191 and Richard six weeks later, whose combined armies tipped the scales in favour of the Christians.

It is not intended to describe each and every phase of the siege between 1189 and the arrival of Philip and Richard which brought the conflict to an end. The fact is that both sides experienced periodic victories but they also experienced sustained hardship, starvation, fever, plague, dysentery, malaria and scurvy on a terrible scale, all of which were aggravated by the heat, flies and dust storms. Whilst the Muslims in the city were able to keep watch from 'The Accursed Tower' (facing landward) and the 'Tower of Flies' (facing the sea), Guy's force spent its time trying to tunnel under their battlements, filling in the city's moat with rocks, bundles of brushwood and dead bodies, and digging a moat and creating defence-works around their own lines. Relieving fleets were destroyed in the harbour, monumental siege towers were built and occasionally destroyed by strategically located mangonel from within the city, and the crusaders responded with balistas and trebuchet, two of which they used with particular accuracy, which were known as 'God's own catapult' and the 'Evil Neighbour'. Missiles, which rained down on the city, by day and by night, included rocks, fire bombs, and the carcasses of dead animals and humans, all intended to terrify the inhabitants and spread disease (i.e. an early

St. Thomas of Acon

form of biological warfare) which they undoubtedly did. It is now impossible to imagine the depths of despair, the horrors of daily life, or the number of dead and dying on both sides during the course of this siege, which lasted for nearly two years. Nor is it possible to estimate the total number of casualties, mainly because of the difficulty of distinguishing between deaths in battle and deaths from injury, famine and disease, all complicated, of course, by the unknown factor of the level of desertions. The truth is that we will probably never know the true cost of the siege, although some idea might be obtained from the fact that it has been estimated that a total of 600,000 is said to have been involved. What we *do* know is that – on the Christian side alone – the dead included Queen Silbylla of Jerusalem and her two daughters, together with 6 archbishops, 12 bishops, 40 earls or counts, 500 barons (or great nobles) and 'a host of common-folk whose number cannot be counted' (Stubbs).

Eventually, of course, the defenders of Acre were worn down and, on 4th July 1191, made an offer of surrender which was refused, although one week later, after another failed attack by Saladin, their surrender was accepted. Tragically, one further act of barbarism was to follow which for ever tarnished the reputation of King Richard. It seems that the terms of the surrender included the exchange of 2,700 Saracen prisoners for 1,600 Christians, the payment of 200,000 Saracen talents, and the return of the 'true Cross of Christ' captured by Saladin at the Battle of Hattin. Which of these was the last straw is not clear but, for some reason, during the course of these proceedings, Richard became totally enraged and ordered that the 2,700 Muslim prisoners be slaughtered, and this was promptly carried out in full view of the defeated garrison. The horror of such an act is almost unimaginable today but, with this final act of barbarity, the siege of Acre came to an end and the city thereafter became the capital of what was left of the Crusader Kingdom and remained so for another hundred years. (Author's note: It must be added that, in recent times, alternative theories have been advanced for Richard's apparent display of cruelty which centre around the possibility that, given that he was going to leave Acre within days, he had no choice as far as his captives were concerned, being unable to take them with him or leave them behind. His solution, it has been argued, was to add to his reputation for ruthlessness by slaughtering them.)

The Siege of Acre was a victory for the crusading kings, but one which appeared to totally satiate any further interest Philip might

The Crusades

have had in conflict with Saladin and, soon after, ostensibly in the interests of his health, he returned to France, leaving his army under the command of the Duke of Burgundy.

Richard and Saladin were to face each other twice more; once in August 1191, when their armies met at Arsuf in an indecisive battle in which Saladin lost 7,000 men, and again in the Spring of 1192, when Richard, with a smaller force, defeated him at the Battle of Jaffa. The myth of Saladin's invincibility was thereby exposed but, by then, Richard had already been in the field too long and was being troubled by reports he was receiving concerning his brother (John) in England. He and Saladin therefore entered into a truce whereby the Crusader Kingdom was limited to a narrow coastal strip, but Christians were allowed open access to Jerusalem, and Richard went home satisfied, bringing the 3rd Crusade to an end. He made no attempt to capture or visit Jerusalem and so far as is known, he and Saladin never met. As is well known, en route to England, Richard was captured by Leopold V of Austria and held for ransom for two years. On his release King Philip of France, his one-time ally, is said to have written to John in England, warning him to 'Look to yourself; the devil is loose.'

CHAPTER 7

After the Siege

As experienced following the capture of Jerusalem nearly a hundred years earlier, the end of hostilities at Acre once again brought military Orders to the fore. At the end of the 1st Crusade three Orders had emerged from the chaos to assist in returning Jerusalem to a state of normality, namely the Hospitallers, Templars, and the Order of Saint Lazarus. Following the Siege of Acre it was those same Orders which, once again, shouldered the burden except that, on that occasion, they were assisted by two new Orders, i.e. the Teutonic Knights and the Order of Saint Thomas of Acon, both of which had been formed during the Siege and, at one point, had shared a tower awarded them by King Guy of Jerusalem. To assist in distinguishing between their various areas of activity, therefore, this might be an appropriate point at which to explain that, in addition to their role as warrior/crusaders, the Hospitallers looked after the sick and injured; the Templars protected pilgrims; the Order of Saint Lazarus cared for and, to a certain extent, consisted of lepers; the Teutonic Order tended the Germans; and the Order of Saint Thomas of Acon was founded to serve the English, and especially for the distasteful task of burying the dead.

It is not intended to go into detail concerning the origins of those Orders, or the nature of their daily round (other than to explain that it mainly consisted of services, prayers, the care of weapons, clothing and animals, and such others duties as their superiors might expect of them), but to confine the remainder of this chapter solely to the Order of Saint Thomas of Acon, because it was that which – centuries later - attracted the attention of John Walker and led to his founding a masonic Order to commemorate its ideals and activities. First, however, it is proposed to clarify the term 'military Order'.

St. Thomas of Acon

A military Order, which should not be confused with a monarchical, honorific or religious Order, was a confraternity of warriors who were prepared to jettison all personal interests and aspirations and take a solemn obligation to spend the rest of their lives in company with those of a like disposition, living in poverty, chastity, obedience and prayer, in pursuit of some common objective. Besides catering for their basic daily needs of food and shelter, it uniquely combined to the satisfaction of its members, the monastic and chivalric ways of life. Membership invariably involved being granted Papal or Royal recognition, the wearing of regalia and, in the case of those Orders formed in the Holy Land, their 'common objective' was the expulsion of Muslims in the name of Christianity. In the words of St. Bernard of Clairvaux, who reconciled the Knights Templar with the idea of 'killing in the name of God', a military Order was: 'A new kind of knighthood, and one unknown to ages gone by. It ceaselessly wages a two-fold war both against flesh and blood and against a spiritual army of evil in the heavens'. An objective to be desired, he asserted, was to die in battle in the name of the Lord or, as he explained it, 'If they are blessed who die *in* the Lord, how much more are they who die *for* the Lord.' That having been clarified, we can now return to the subject of the Order of St. Thomas of Acon and the evidence for an existence which lasted for over three hundred years.

It is only fair to point out that, over the years, a variety of theories have been put forward to account for the origins of the Order of St. Thomas of Acon, the three most common of which have been that: It was founded by Becket's sister and her husband Thomas Fitz Theobald de Helles (see below) in London ; or by Henry II, who made a vow to provide two hundred knights for the Holy Land when he was absolved from guilt for Becket's murder; or by Richard the Lionheart, who is said to have been saved from shipwreck in 1190 by an apparition of St. Thomas.

Despite the plausibility of those claims, it is now generally accepted that the Order of Saint Thomas of Acon was founded during the Siege of Acre in 1191, and support for that statement is provided by:

Matthew Paris, a 13th century Benedictine monk who not only referred to the Order in his chronicles of the period, but produced a map of Acre after the Siege showing the position of the Hospital of St. Thomas of Acre.

After the Siege

Bishop Thomas Tanner who, in his *Notitia Monastica*, wrote that the Order 'was about this time (i.e.the 13th century) instituted in the Holy Land, viz: Militiae Hospitalis St. Thomas Martyris Cantariensis de Acon, being a branch of the Templars.' (quoted in Sir William Dugdale's *Monasticon Anglicanum* Vol VI, p.645)

William Maitland who quoted Roger Twysden's *Decem Scriptores* in which it is explained that 'When the City of Acars or Acon, in the Holy Land (called also Ptolemais) was besieged by the Christians, one William, an Englishman by nation, being chaplain to Radulphus de Diceto, Dean of London, when he went to Jerusalem bound himself by a vow that if he should prosperously enter Acon he would build a chapel to St. Thomas the Martyr at his own charge, according to his ability, and would procure there, to the honour of the said martyr, a churchyard to be consecrated which was done.'(*History of London* Vol. II, p.886, 1756)

Hugh Clark who wrote that 'King Richard the First of England, instituted this Order after the surprizal of the city of Acon. It consisted of the English Nation. Their Patron was Saint Thomas Becket, Archbishop of Canterbury. Their Garment white, and the ensign of the Order was a red cross charged in the centre with a white Escallop shell.'(*A concise history of knighthood* Vol I, p.167, 1784)

Professor W. Stubbs who, In a lecture given in 1878, explained that 'Amongst these was one little known and obscure knightly order, which Englishmen need not be ashamed to recognise; the Order of the Knights of St. Thomas of Acre. This was a little body of men who had formed themselves into a semi-religious order on the model of the Hospitallers. In the third Crusade, one William, an English priest, chaplain to Ralph de Diceto, Dean of St. Paul's, had devoted himself to the work of burying the dead at Acre, as the Hospitallers had given themselves at first to the work of tending the sick. He had built himself a little chapel there, and bought ground for a cemetery; like a thorough Londoner of the period, he had called it after St. Thomas the Martyr; and, somehow or other, as his design was better known, the family of the martyr seem to have approved of it; the brother-in-law and sister of Becket became founders and benefactors, and a

St. Thomas of Acon

Hospital of St. Thomas the Martyr of Acre was built in London itself on the site of the house where the martyr was born.' (*The Medieval kingdoms of Cyprus and Armenia,* 1878)

John Watney who wrote that: 'The order of St. Thomas was instituted by the King of England, Richard, surnamed Coeur de Lyon, after the surprizal of Acars, and being of the English nation they held the rule of St. Augustin, and wore a white habit and a full red cross, charged in the middle with a white scallop. They took for their patron the Archbishop of Canterbury, the Metropolitan of England, Thomas a Becket, who suffered martyrdom (as his favourers say) under the King of England, Henry II of that name'. He also added that 'The chronicles of the Teutonic Knights, in relating the capture of Acre in 1191, places the Knights of St. Thomas at the head of the 5,000 men whom the King of England sent into the Holy Land.' (*Some account of the Hospital of St. Thomas of Acon in the Cheap, London, and of the Plate of the Mercers' Company,* 1892)

Jean Imray, Archivist of the Mercer's Company, who prepared a pamphlet commemorating the 800th Anniversary of the Martyrdom of St. Thomas Becket in which she wrote that 'The order was certainly established in Acre, or Acon, some time before 1200. Its rule was similar to that of the Knights Templar and its aim was to provide succour and hospitality for poor pilgrims on their way to the Holy Land, to relieve poor and infirm persons who sought its aid and to collect alms for the ransom of Christian captives in the hands of the Turks for which, like the Templars, it had a special indulgence from the Pope'. (*Thomas Becket, the Mercers' Company and the City of London,* 1970)

Dr. A.J.Forey who wrote that 'The Order of St. Thomas of Acon was founded by William, an Englishman and Chaplain to Ralph de Diceto, the Dean of St. Paul's Cathedral in London, because of a vow he had made during his sea-voyage to the Holy Land, when he was beset on his journey by the common dread of the sea.' (*The military order of St. Thomas of Acre,* in the English Historical Review, No. CCCLXIV, July 1977)

Desmond Seward who wrote that 'About this time another order was emerging, the Hospitallers of St. Thomas of Canterbury at Acre, usually called Knights of St. Thomas Acon. During the siege of Acre,

After the Siege

William, chaplain to the dean of St. Paul's, moved by the English crusaders' misery, began nursing the sick and wounded. After the city's capture, aided by King Richard, he built a small chapel and purchased a cemetery, founding a hospital and a nursing brotherhood restricted to Englishmen.' (*The Monks of War*, p.60, 1972)

D.J.Keene and V.Harding who, in their *Historical gazetteer of London before the Great Fire* (1987) stated that 'The order of St. Thomas of Acre was established in the Holy Land at the time of the third crusade, when the cult of Becket was spreading rapidly throughout Europe. In the 1220s the order was re-established according to the military rule of the Teutonic knights, and in 1227-8 it acquired as a site for a church the land in St. Mary Colechurch parish where Becket had been born'.

William Page, editor of 'A history of the County of London' in which it is explained that the hospital of St. Thomas of Acon was founded in honour of St. Mary and St. Thomas of Canterbury for a master and brethren of the military order of St. Thomas the Martyr by Thomas Fitz Theobald de Helles, whose wife Agnes was a sister of the murdered archbishop. (*A History of the County of London: Volume 1: London within the Bars, Westminster and Southwark* (1909) pp.491-95)

(Author's note: The importance of this quotation is that it supports the view that, if a hospital was formed *for* an Order, that Order must already have existed and, together with the other quotations, clearly negates any suggestion that the Order was originally founded in London. It should also be added that recent research has indicated that the Thomas de Helles who founded the hospital was not the husband of Becket's sister, but her heir, and either her son or her nephew.)

Having, therefore, established that the Order was founded in Acre in 1191 by William, chaplain to the Dean of St. Paul's, who is thought to have been one of the five thousand who travelled to the Holy Land with Baldwin, Archbishop of Canterbury, as part of Richard's army, its subsequent progress was constant but undramatic. It is known, for instance, that:

St. Thomas of Acon

In 1207 a messenger from the Order travelled to England to seek the assistance of King John in raising money for the redemption of Christian captives in the Holy Land, and that on 13th October 1207 King John gave that messenger a letter of safe conduct.

Until the 1220s, the Order in Acre consisted of canons, who devoted themselves to the burial of the dead, the care of the poor, and ransoming captives.

Soon after that, the Order's role changed, with the arrival in Acre of two warlike Bishops, Peter des Roches, Bishop of Winchester, and William Briwere, Bishop of Exeter, both of whom were temporarily out of favour at Court in England. Peter des Roche had led a division of the royal army at the Battle of Lincoln in 1217, was the guardian of King Henry III, and served as Grand Justiciary of England. He is known to have built a Priory at Selborne, and several monasteries and churches in England and France. In 1228-9, however, he and Briwere were on crusade in Acre with Frederick II, the Holy Roman Emperor, and that is where he encountered (or re-encountered) the Order of St. Thomas of Acon, to whom he gave a new (and larger) church, five hundred marks (a large sum in those days) and urged them to follow the rule of the Teutonic Knights. (Author's note: It is thought possible that Peter des Roche may already have been acquainted with the Order of St. Thomas of Acon before reaching Acre, since it was he who completed the building of the new London bridge started by Peter de Colechurch in 1176, and the Order of St. Thomas ultimately became responsible for the administration of the funds of that bridge, as will be explained in Chapter 8. He also re-endowed and moved to a more favourable location on the river, the famous hospital in Southwark, significantly known as St. Thomas's Hospital.)

In 1278 King Edward I of England, who led the relatively insignificant 9th Crusade to Acre, wrote a letter to King Hugh III of Cyprus and Jerusalem, commending Ralph de Coumbe, the Master and brethren of the hospital of St. Thomas of Acre. (Edward seems to have had a particularly soft spot for both Acre and the Order of St. Thomas of Acon and is said to have endowed the Order generously. Two of his daughters were born in Acre, one of whom bore the name 'Joan of Acre'. It is also known that, after his return to England, he carried out extensive work on the Tower of London and that 'The engineer who redesigned the Tower's moat, Brother John of the Order of St. Thomas of Acre, had clearly been recruited in the East' (Wikipedia, *'Edward I of England'*, p.3).

After the Siege

In 1291 Acre was once again under siege, this time by a Mameluke army under Sultan Qalawun. On this occasion, however, the Christian forces did not prevail and, according to Seward (*Monks of War*, 1972, p.90) all the Hospitallers and Templars who had remained were either killed or taken captive, whilst all but one of the Teutonic Knights, and all nine of the brethren of St. Thomas and twenty-five Knights of St. Lazarus, were killed, resulting in the loss of the city and of the last surviving remnant of the Christian Kingdom of Jerusalem.

For a time the Hospitallers and Templars maintained a presence in Cyprus, although the Hospitallers later moved to Rhodes and adopted a maritime role. Having lost all its Knights at Acre, what was left of the Order of St. Thomas also based itself in Cyprus, at first in Kolossi, but later in Nicosia, where it established itself at a former 6th century Byzantine church which, under their care, became the church of St. Nicholas Anglicorum (i.e. of the English). (Author's note: Interestingly, after Cyprus fell to the Ottomans, the church of St. Nicholas Anglicorum was the only church in Cyprus allowed to retain its bells.)

During the course of the move to Cyprus, it would seem the Prior of the Order, who had hitherto been regarded as its head, lost that role which, thereafter, was assumed by the Master in Nicosia who claimed the right to be regarded as the 'Master of the whole Order of the Knighthood of St. Thomas in the Kingdoms of Cyprus, Apulia, Sicily, Brundusium, England, Flanders, Brabant, Scotland, Wales, Ireland and Cornwall', although that claim was not necessarily accepted in London, with the result that it became something of an issue and was not finally settled until 1379 when it was agreed that the Grand Master of the Order would be the Master of the Hospital of St. Thomas of Acon in London. Having said that, there is some evidence that it had been generally accepted before then because, on 30th August 1344, the head of the Order in Nicosia wrote a letter as 'Grand Preceptor' (indicating 'Provincial' status) authorising two of his Knights to collect money in behalf of the Order. And on the 2nd February 1357, Sir Richard de Tykehill, an English chaplain from the diocese of York, was admitted to the Order in Cyprus in a ceremony conducted by Hugh de Courteys, who was similarly described as Preceptor, in the church of St. Nicholas Anglicorum. That ceremony was witnessed by Francis de Gave, a burgess of Nicosia; Sir Robert of Swillington, canon; Sir Richard of Chatesby, an English priest; and

St. Thomas of Acon

William Gaston of England, who was Turcopolier to the King of Cyprus. It was the last known admission to the Order in Cyprus or, indeed, anywhere else in the Middle East.

Thereafter the Order faded away in the Mediterranean and, with the dissolution of the Templars, the move of the Hospitallers to Rhodes, the relocation of the Teutonic Knights to Venice and then to Prussia, and the end of the Order of St. Lazarus as a fighting force, all further interest in crusading came to an end.

Little is known of the Order of St. Thomas of Acon in Cyprus after the fall of the Latin Kingdom, and it can only be assumed that its members either died, moved elsewhere, joined other Orders, or returned to England. It must be remembered that they were never numerous.

One thing is certain. The Order did not die at that time, and proof of that is provided by the fact that, from time to time, it has occasionally reappeared, usually in Jacobite circles in Europe but also in 18th century Scotland. None of that, fortunately, is anything to do with this account, the next task of which is to consider the Order's translation to London.

CHAPTER 8

The Order in London

The Order of St. Thomas of Acon enjoyed three-and-a-half centuries of relative stability in London, that is to say, when contrasted with its experience in the Holy Land where, to all intents and purposes, it had been engaged in a constant state of war. Either because of the patronage of successive kings; the influence of the Becket-cult ; or because of the will of the people, who regarded Becket as 'one of their own', it rapidly became popular and important to the City of London which, it must be remembered, pre-dates Parliament as a legal entity. Traces of it would probably have been there today had not Henry VIII taken a dislike to and, in 1538, dissolved all the monasteries and priories in the kingdom, but especially those dedicated to St. Thomas, irrespective of whether that 'Thomas' was either St. Thomas à Becket or St. Thomas More.

By far the most important factor in promoting that stability and popularity, was the decision by Agnes, the sister of Becket, to donate the family home in Ironmonger Lane, for the purposes of erecting a hospital and chapel, for a Master and twelve members of the Order, to the memory of her brother, a decision carried into effect in 1227-8 by Thomas de Helles, who was either her nephew or son but, more importantly, the executor of her Will. This is not to suggest that building began immediately, although a hospital and chapel may have been in existence soon after that date, because it is known that space had been made available for that purpose by Peter, the architect/priest of the chapel of St. Mary Colechurch, which stood nearby at the junction of Poultry and the south end of Old Jewry in Cheapside, and it is known that members of the Order were in residence between 1231 and 1241. (Author's note: Peter de Colechurch is known to have been kindly disposed towards Becket and the Order and, after being commissioned to rebuild London

St. Thomas of Acon

bridge in stone, he made a point of locating a church at its centre, dedicated to the Martyr and, after his death in 1205, was himself interred in the crypt of that church.)

It was not until June 1248 that a papal bull was issued authorising the fraternity to construct their own chapel, followed in 1249 by permission to use a plot of land nearby as a cemetery. Thereafter progress was rapid and, when completed, the church of St. Thomas of Acon is said to have been a 'large and noble structure, with a choir, a nave, and side aisles', with its main entrance in Cheapside which (according to Charles Dickens Jr.) "remains what it was five centuries ago, the greatest thoroughfare in the City of London" (*Dickens's Dictionary of London,* 1879). Two great churches dominated that thoroughfare, which was used for a variety of purposes, including State processions, and they were St. Paul's at one end and the church of St. Thomas of Acon at the other.

The hospital and church grew steadily thereafter, mostly as a result of gifts (such as those from the king and other leading members of society), alms, donations to maintain a chantry (i.e. An endowment to sing mass for someone's soul), gifts in frankalmoigne (i.e.In return for prayers said for the soul of the donor and his heirs), and the customary activities of priests and brothers in singing dirges and saying mass at obit (i.e. At the death, or the anniversary of someone's death), especially members of the Company of Mercers, who made an annual payment to the Order for that service. One way or another, the Order became increasingly important to the public life of the City, and, as a result of gifts and bequests, it eventually acquired lands and property in Wapping, Stepney, West Ham, Coulsdon (Surrey), Harrow-on-the-Hill, Plumstead, Buckingham, Doncaster (the hospital of St. James), Berkhamstead (the hospital of St. John the Baptist), and enough land and property in and around Cheapside to enable it to enlarge its grounds until it eventually became a substantial complex. Its church bell was adopted as the signal for opening the city gates which were normally locked overnight, and its tolling for Vespers was accepted as the indicator that markets should close. Meetings of various livery companies were held there during the civic year, including those for the resolving of disputes, and it became the custom on certain dates (e.g. All Saints and Holy Innocents) for the mayor and his household to meet at the church of St. Thomas of Acon before going on to St. Paul's for Vespers. By far the most important visit, of course, took place on the 28th October annually, when the Mayor was formally 'sworn' before

The Order in London

the Barons of the Exchequer or the Constable of the Tower, after which he made his way to the church of St. Thomas where he and the aldermen made offerings at the birthplace of St. Thomas. The mayor, aldermen and sheriffs also made processions on Christmas Day, and on 29th December (the day of Thomas's martyrdom) they went there for mass.

The Order continued to play its part in the life of the City until 1538 and the Dissolution of the Monasteries and from a variety of sources (but notably Watney's book on the Hospital) it has been possible to identify the following list of Masters, in each case showing at least one date when the person named is recorded to have been Master:

Henry de Neville, 1243
Ralph Waleys, 1244 and 1248
William de Huntingfeud, 1267
Friar Robert de Conde, Conele or Covelee, 1277
Henry de Dunholm, temp. Edward I
Edmond de London, temp. Edward II
Friar Richard de Bardeley, 1314
Friar Henry de Bedford, 1326
Nicholas de Clifton, 1327
Ralph de Coumbe, 1327
Friar Batholomew de Colchestre, 1333, 1340 and 1344
Friar William Mylem, 1347
Thomas Swallow (died 1371)
Richard Sewell, 1371
Richard Alrede or Aldred, 1391
Friar Bovyn or Bovyngton, 1400 and 1419
John Niel or Neell, 1420, 1428 (died 1463)
John Parker, 1463
John Harding, 1578 (died 1492)
Richard Adams, 1505 (removed 23rd July 1510)
John Yong or Young S.T.P., 1510
Lawrence Gopfelar or Gospelar, 1526

It should not be assumed from this account that the life of the Order in London was without incident, and there were a number of occasions when it found itself in difficulties, some times because of the cost of repairs and maintenance, and some times because of the financial ineptitude of its Masters. In 1279, for instance, it was

St. Thomas of Acon

involved in a dispute with Archbishop Peckham (the Archbishop of Canterbury) over his rights of visitation, and was in danger of sequestration or excommunication. And 1394, when an attempt was made to absorb the Order into the 'Bonhommes' (or Bluefriars) of Ashridge in Hertfordshire, which necessitated an appeal to the Pope to ensure that the Order remained in control of its own destiny. The worst was yet to come, however, and that occurred on 20th October, 1538 on which date the Master and brethren were instructed to surrender the hospital and chapel to the Crown, as part of the Dissolution of the Monasteries. At that time there was only a Master and six brethren in residence, all of whom received pensions. The Master (Lawrence Gopfelar) was granted a pension of £66 13s 4d annually; Thomas Exmewe received £7 6s 8d. annually, Anthony Bradshaw and Humphrey Edward, £6 each annually; and William Dingley, Richard Baker, and Robert Evans, £5 annually. Some of its houses and other properties were then sold-off or sub-let for rent by the Crown, but the church, cloister, vestry, chapter-house, sexton's chamber and churchyard were sold by the king to the Mercers' Company in April 1542, thus ending the history of the Order of St. Thomas of Acon in London.

Before leaving this section, however, it is proposed to say a little more about its penultimate Master, John Yong (or Young) S.T.P., first mentioned in Chapter 1 of this book, but now known to every member of the Order as 'the Vicar of Honey Lane Market' who, in 1510, had to be coerced into accepting its Mastership. That wasn't the actual name of his church, of course, which was All Hallows, Honey Lane, which was one of the eighty-six churches destroyed in the Great Fire of London but was never rebuilt. Had it been so, it would now be found at 114 Cheapside. That having been said, it is worth adding that the selection of Yong as the Master of Acon proved to be an inspired choice and, during his mastership, because of an obvious 'flair for finance', the Order moved from a position of indebtedness to one of solvency, and the Mercers' Company formally accepted the role of its defender and advocate.

Yong was born in 1463 at Newton Longueville, Buckinghamshire, and admitted to Winchester College at the age of eleven, where he remained until 1480. On 1st August 1480 he was elected to a scholarship at New College, Oxford, and two years later succeeded to a Fellowship, only resigning in 1502 on becoming S.T.P. ('Sanctae Theologiae Professor' or 'Doctor of Divinity') and rector at St. Martin's, Oxford. In 1510, whilst serving as parson of All

The Order in London

Hallows, Honey Lane, Cheapside, he was appointed Master of the Order of St. Thomas of Acre but, two years later, was chosen by Dean John Colet of St. Paul's, to be his suffragan bishop which, once again displaying diffidence, he was 'loth to do, for fear to incur the obloquy of the people, and because the office would prevent him from seeing to the profit of the hospital, which he had much intended, and to have the same place kept in good order and prosperity in time to come'. After considerable delay and prevarication, legal advice was sought from Thomas More (who lived nearby in a house rented from the Order), and the opinion of the Pope was sought, the net result of which was that on 3rd July 1514 he was consecrated suffragan bishop of London and assumed the title of Bishop of Gallipoli. He died on 28th March 1525 and is buried in New College, Oxford, where his grave can be seen to this day. It is covered by a monumental brass, which is described in the Rev.C. Boutell's *'Monumental brasses of England'* (1849).

Dean John Colet, who chose John Yong to be the Master of the Order, is perhaps now best remembered as the founder of St. Paul's School in 1509. He located the school within the Acon complex, and placed its administration in the hands of the Mercers' Company. The boys' school eventually moved to Barnes, London and the girls' school to Brook Green, London. The Foundation has a wholly owned subsidiary which, interestingly, is called 'Acon Investments Limited'.

CHAPTER 9

In retrospect

Having explained when and where the original Order of St. Thomas of Acon came into existence but was eventually dissolved, and the circumstances under which, hundreds of years later, a group of friends meeting in Blackheath decided that it had been created for the most worthy of reasons and that, being uniquely English in origin but seemingly forgotten, it deserved to be revived and commemorated, it only remains to account for three questions, which are:

Why it was decided to commemorate it within freemasonry;
Why, after 1998, it expanded so quickly; and....
What was the secret of its success.

The answer to the first is that a common bond existed between the founders of the new Order in that they were all freemasons, who were accustomed to meeting on a regular basis in a house in Blackheath, in order to sustain, for academic reasons, the ceremonies of a number of small and obscure masonic Orders and Societies which might otherwise have faded into history. More importantly, at some point in their masonic careers, they had all discovered an interest in the Crusades as a consequence of which each of them had joined the 'Religious, Military and Masonic Order of the Temple', i.e. the Templars, which should not be confused with the 'Sovereign Military Order of the Temple of Jerusalem', which is also 'Templar' but has no connection to freemasonry. The masonic version is an independent organization in which the Christian religion, a willingness to replicate the dress and customs of Knights Templar, and observe what they regard as Templar 'precepts', are the fundamental characteristics.

St. Thomas of Acon

Following the chance discovery by John Walker of the long-forgotten military Order, he described it to his brother-masons who, like him, were attracted by those aspects described in Chapter 1, but especially its English character so, out of academic interest and a sort of quiet patriotism, they decided to revive it on a limited basis, and to work what they could trace of its ceremonies within a masonic context. This presented no difficulty, because they already had a place to meet, most of the equipment necessary, the knowledge and skills to adapt medieval ritual to the present day, and a desire to do so. In short, the seeds of the new Order provided by Walker could not have fallen onto more fertile ground.

There are several reasons why it should have expanded so rapidly after 1998, the most obvious of which is because of 'pent-up demand'. It must be remembered that although, by then, they had already been meeting for twenty-five years, until that date membership of the Order had been restricted by the size of the temple in Andrew Stephenson's house. Once it was decided to re-locate to larger premises, that constraint came to an end and, with it, any further limitation on numbers. The result was instantaneous and, from that point on, ten, twenty or even thirty candidates at a time became the norm and a few members (e.g. John Bray, Gordon Gentry and Keith Ansell) found themselves scurrying around the masonic-world (in the UK and overseas) fulfilling the duties of Worthy Master wherever and whenever they were required, so as to help members, and prospective members, form chapels of their own. Others suddenly found themselves taking part in consecrating teams, and the administrative burden, especially on successive Grand Secretaries, became enormous. In all probability they did not look at it as a burden, and probably regarded it as an exciting period of intense activity in which it was a privilege to be involved.

Another possible reason for its rapid expansion, and one which its critics might suggest, could have been because it was 'new'. Freemasonry can certainly be a lifelong preoccupation, and most of its members are unquestionably mature in years, but that is no reason for thinking they are any different from everyone else in enjoying the novelty of being involved in something 'new', so it is possible that its newness may have been one of its attractions, although it is doubtful if this was the case for more than a handful of its new members.

An alternative explanation, and the one the author prefers, is because it answered a 'need'. Freemasonry is usually described as

In retrospect

a 'peculiar system of morality, veiled in allegory and illustrated by symbols' but, given the vagueness of that description, and the difficulty of interpreting allegories, it can sometimes take a lifetime for its members to come to terms with either its origins or what it is all about. For some, that is one of its appeals although, for others, it can be exasperating. Any wonder, therefore, that when a new Order appears on the scene, the ritual of which carries a Christian message, is easy to understand, and the history of which can be proved to be true, it should be welcomed with open arms. Such was certainly the case with Acon, the emergence of which, for many, was as welcome as a lifeline to a drowning man.

The secret of the Order's appeal is even easier to explain and arises from two things; the fact that it commemorates the only military Order involved in the Crusades known to have been entirely English in origin, and the simple Christian-message behind its ritual.

To be specific, the man who formed the original medieval Order was English by name and English by nature. He is known to history as 'William the Englishman', and he was the chaplain to the Dean of St. Paul's in London. The Order was legitimised by one of England's most famous kings, Richard the Lionheart, who wore a red crusader cross, the flag of England, to distinguish him in battle, and whose armorial standard bore the three lions which are known to everyone who has ever cheered for an English sports team. Finally, the Order became distinguished in battle under the command of the Bishop of Winchester, and took its name from England's most well-known and iconic religious figure, St.Thomas à Becket.

The Order's Christian message (which is best understood by referring to the Gospel of St. Matthew Chapter 25, vs.34-40) is conveyed to all candidates by their being challenged on four separate occasions to demonstrate their willingness to help those less fortunate than themselves; by proving their willingness to 'collect alms in the cause of knightly charity'; by promising to consider all charitable claims made on them and respond if the claim is worthy and they are able to assist; and finally, by making at least one pilgrimage to Canterbury Cathedral to visit the place where St. Thomas was martyred.

These, then, are the answers to the three questions posed at the start of this chapter. In retrospect, there is possibly a fourth, which is: Given the modest nature of its beginnings, would John Walker have approved of the expansion of the Order and the

St. Thomas of Acon

changes which have been necessary to enable it to take its place alongside the other masonic Orders and Societies?

Unfortunately, that is a question the answer to which we will never know. There are, however, two things of which we can be sure, which are: More people than he can ever have imagined are now aware of the one-time existence of a small English military Order, known as the Order of St. Thomas of Acon, formed during the Siege of Acre, and the name of the man whose researches led to its recension, John Edward Nowell Walker.

Requiescat in pace, Brother John. Few are privileged to bequeath such a legacy!

APPENDIX I

KNIGHTS HUMILITAS and KNIGHTS CARITAS
Showing year of appointment

Knights Humilitas
Rt. Rev'd Bishop. G.F.Crane	2004
D.C.Kibble-Rees	2005
B.Clarke	2006

Knights Caritas
J.W.Mitchell	2004
L.N.Bale	2005
J.A.Loat	2005
B.N.Long	2007
B.F.Uttley	2007

APPENDIX II

GRAND OFFICERS (Active ranks only)

Name	Year Apptd.	Name	Year Apptd.
Grand Master		**Grand Prior**	
J.E.N.Walker	1974	D.H.G.Bourke (Rev)	1998
A.B.Stephenson	1991	G.J.Crane (Rt.Rev)	2000
B.Clarke	1997	B.N.Long	2007
D.Kibble-Rees	2003		
Grand Marshal		**Grand Treasurer**	
B.F.Catt	1998	A.Perry	1998
H.F.Doe	1999	D.Kibble-Rees	1999
K.Ansell	2000	B.F.Uttley	2003
D.K.Rhodes	2003	D.Shooter	2007
D.Newton	2004		
J.J.Field	2007		
Grand Registrar		**Grand Secretary**	
W.A.J.Thompson	2004	J.W.Mitchell	1998
P.Layton	2005	J.H.Bray	2002
A.Temple	2007	J.Loat	2003
Grand Historian		**Deputy Grand Marshal**	
L.S.G.White	2003	H.F.Doe	1998
		K.Ansell	1999
		D.K.Rhodes	2002
		D.Newton	2003
		J.J.Field	2005
		S.Polkinghorne	2007
Grand Almoner		**Grand Sword Bearer**	
G.M.Gentry	2000	G.M.Gentry	1999
D.J.Price	2003	D.J.Price	2000
J.R.Richardson	2004	W.A.J.Thompson	2003
J.Paternoster	2005	D.A.Hope	2004
P.T.Coles	2007	G.A.G.Barker	2007
Deputy Grand Secretary		**Grand Banner Bearer**	
J.H.Bray	2000	D.J.Price	1999
J.A.Loat	2002	D.A.Hope	2003
P.Layton	2003	D.B.Saunders	2004
R.C.Leske-Heed	2004	J.Paternoster	2005
R.Williamson	2007	R.Eaves	2006
		G.Peacock	2007

APPENDIX II (CONTD.)

Assistant Grand Marshal
D.Newton	2000
D.B.Saunders	2002
L.R.Haslam	2003
J.J.Field	2004
A.Llewellyn	2005
J.Monkhouse	2005
P.T.Coles	2006
B.Bailes	2007
R.Foster	2007

Assistant Grand Secretary
R.C.Leske-Heed	2003
B.Howarth	2005
P.Mycock	2007

Grand Herald
D.B.Saunders	2000
W.A.J.Thompson	2001
G.A.Cooper	2002
R.Eaves	2004
G.A.G.Barker	2005
G.Peacock	2006
B.J.Prevett	2007

Grand Organist
A.B.Stephenson	1998
J.R.Paternoster	2002
G.Hewitt	2004
D.M.Davies	2007

Grand Doorkeeper
K.Ansell	1998
W.A.J.Thompson	2000
D.Hope	2002
J.Richardson	2003
M.G.Harridine	2004
B.Lobb	2005
J.McLain	2006
N.D.Williams	2007

Grand Sentry
G.M.Gentry	1998
L.S.G.White	1999
S.Smith	2002

Grand Cellarer
J.H.Bray	1999
L.N.Bale	2002
F.E.Allen	2003
M.Dupee	2003
A.E.Lovas	2003
P.C.Wilmink	2003
T.King	2005
R.L.Harrison	2006
E.Adams	2007
C.Boughton	2007
J.Busic	2007
R.Neff	2007
W.M.Millane	2007

APPENDIX III

GRAND PRECEPTORS OF PROVINCES
Showing the year of appointment

Yorkshire & the East Midlands Counties
J.H.Bray 2002
B.H.Long 2003
A.W.Llewellyn 2006

London & the South Eastern Counties
D.C.Kibble-Rees 2003
M.G.Harridine 2003

North Western & West Midland Counties *
L.N.Bale 2003

East Anglia
K.Ansell 2003
R.C.Leske-Heed 2006

Lancashire
D.K.Rhodes 2004

Australia & New Zealand
K.Henderson 2005

United States of America
A.E.Lovas 2005

Cheshire & North Wales
J.D.McLain 2007

Canada
T.King 2007

Central Midlands
D.A.Hope 2007

South Wales
G.C.Royle 2008

* Province closed on re-organization in 2007

APPENDIX IV

PROVINCES OF THE ORDER
Showing the date of Consecration

Yorkshire & East Midland Counties	23.11.02
London & the South Eastern Counties	29.03.03
North Western & West Midland Counties *	02.08.03
East Anglia	20.09.03
Lancashire	30.07.04
Australia & New Zealand	16.08.05
United States of America	11.09.05
Cheshire & North Wales	26.02.07
Canada	14.07.07
Central Midlands	28.07.07
South Wales	14.06.08

* Subsequently re-organised as the Province of Cheshire & North Wales

APPENDIX V

CHAPELS OF THE ORDER
in numerical order

Name	Location	Date
Blackheethe T. I.	London	Unknown
Becket the Martyr No. 1	Southend-on-Sea	29.08.98
The Pilgrims' No. 2	Chingford	29.05.99
John o'Gaunt No. 3	Leyland	10.04.99
Richard Coeur de Lion No. 4	Dewsbury	19.06.99
St.Nicholas Anglicorum No .5	Carnforth	05.02.00
Prior William No. 6	Macclesfield	20.05.00
Canterbury No. 7	Canterbury	27.11.99
Coeur de Lion No. 8	Kenton	22.05.00
Hugues D'Avranches No. 9	Chester	19.08.00
Sir Richard de Tykehill No. 10	York	26.08.00
Pilgrim No. 11	Pittsburgh, USA	17.02.00
Trinity No. 12	Washington, USA	17.02.00
The Holy Innocent No. 13	Birmingham	29.04.00
Bishop Hugh de Puiset No.14	Chester-le-Street	28.10.00
Upper Canada No. 15	Peterborough	10.07.00
Edmund, King and Martyr No.16	Great Yarmouth	20.01.01
Robert de Ferrers No. 17	Duffield	29.08.01
Sir Guichard d'Angle No. 18	Aldridge	19.05.01
Thomas à Becket No. 19	Middlesborough	17.11.01
Acre Chapel No. 20	Leeds	23.06.01
Ednyfed Fychan No. 21	Llanfairfechan	01.12.01
St. John No. 22	Eastbourne	26.10.01
St. James of Compostela No. 23	Redditch	19.07.02
Sir Robert de Belesme No. 24	Mansfield	10.08.02
Orme's Chirche No. 25	Ormskirk	31.08.02
De Clare of St. Augustine No.26	Clare	04.01.03
St. Martin's No. 27	Liskeard	01.02.03
Sir Richard de Lucy No. 28	Harlow	12.07.03
Roger de Poitou No. 29	Burnley	28.08.03
Tahoma No. 30	Tacoma, USA	29.10.04
Gerald de Barri No. 31	Penarth	31.01.04
Sir Rice Mansel of Margam No. 32	Port Talbot	27.02.04
St. Cuthbert No. 33	Ashington	29.05.04
Humanitas No. 34	Rojales, Spain	01.05.04
St. Paul No. 35	Melbourne, Australia	21.08.04
St. Stephen No. 36	Perth, Australia	28.08.04
Henry Bolingbroke No. 37	Widnes	17.07.04
William de Teverey No. 38	Long Eaton	02.10.04

APPENDIX V (CONTD.)

Graveley No. 39	Radlett	05.02.05
Sir Rhys ap Thomas No. 40	Carmarthen	28.02.05
King Offa No. 41	Chepstow	02.04.05
St. Andrew No. 42	Sydney, Australia	06.08.05
Nutfield No. 43	Redhill	18.06.05
Dr. George M. Patrick No. 44	Brazos, USA	11.09.05
Lone Star No. 45	Houston, USA	11.09.05
St. John No. 46	Brisbane, Australia	13.08.05
Tejas No. 47	Austin, USA	11.09.05
The Chough No. 48	Auckland, New Zealand	20.08.05
Sir Robert de Bingham No. 49	Nottingham	08.10.05
King Anna No. 50	Newmarket	29.10.05
Novum Eboracum No. 51	New York, USA	17.12.05
Saint David No. 52	Fishguard	04.03.06
Shute No. 53	Monroe, USA	19.03.06
Texas No. 54	San Antonio, USA	28.05.06
Friary Park No. 55	Chichester	28.10.06
Immanuel No. 56	Columbia, USA	19.08.06
Mountaineer No. 57	Morgantown, USA	16.09.06
St. Paul's No. 58	Wokingham	24.02.07
Boadicea No. 59	Tollesbury	31.03.07
Osric No. 60	Gloucester	03.02.07
St. Mary Magdalene No. 61	Warwick	12.03.07
Fort Worth No. 62	Fort Worth, USA	30.06.07
Geoffrey Chaucer No. 63	Gillingham	31.03.07
City of London No. 64	London	31.03.07
Crusader No. 65	Orlando, USA	04.08.07
York No. 66	Mississauga, Canada	14.07.07
Saskatchewan No. 67	Regina, Canada	14.07.07
Robert de la Zouch No. 68	Ashby-de-la-Zouch	20.10.07
St. Luke No. 69	Melbourne, Australia	16.10.07
Ohio No. 70	Delaware, USA	15.03.08
St. Boniface No. 71	Crediton	23.02.08
King Henry V No. 72	Manchester	20.09.08
St. Peter No. 73	Adelaide, Australia	29.11.08
Reginald Fitzjocelyn No. 74	Bath	02.08.08
Clarendon No. 75	Watford	19.07.08
St. Mark No. 76	Stawall, Australia	27.11.08
The Jordan No. 77	Allentown, USA	14.09.08

POSTSCRIPT

Anyone wishing to obtain a 'feel' for the Order of St. Thomas of Acon in London, might find it rewarding to visit the site of the old London Bridge and undertake the short walk described below.

Start from Sir Christopher Wren's famous Monument to the Great Fire of London (easily approached from either Bank or Monument underground stations) and begin to cross the Bridge. Almost immediately, take the steps on your left leading down to Lower Thames Street, and visit the church of St. Magnus the Martyr nearby, because therein you will find an excellent model of the 13th century bridge, which shows the church of St. Thomas of Acon as it must have looked when it was built. The bridge and church was started by Peter de Colechurch, who was a priest-architect whose own church was that of St. Mary Colechurch in Cheapside, which figures prominently in the history of St. Thomas and his family. At one time, Brethren of the Chapel of St. Thomas administered the funds raised from those using the bridge. The church of St. Thomas on the bridge would have been regularly visited by pilgrims making their way towards Canterbury, especially those wishing to give thanks for being able to cross the bridge, most people in those days being frightened of any open expanse of water, because of their common inability to swim.

Once you have seen the model, retrace your steps and begin to cross the bridge towards Southwark. As you do so, you will see the Tower of London on your left. It was a Brother of St. Thomas of Acon, it will be recalled, who was brought from Acre to redesign the Moat surrounding the Tower, on the orders of King Edward I.

At the south end of the bridge (near to the Southwark Needle) you will see Colechurch House, named after the architect of the bridge,

Postscript

who donated part of his own church (St. Mary Colechurch in Cheapside) so as to provide a hospital and chapel for the Order in London.

On the opposite side of the road you will see Southwark Cathedral, and on your left is St. Thomas's Street. Peter des Roche (who gave generously to the Order of St. Thomas of Acon when in Acre) was the Bishop of Winchester, whose seat was at Southwark Cathedral, and it was he who moved the Hospital of St. Thomas to where St. Thomas's Street is today, because the air was 'cooler and sweeter' at that point. It was later moved again, to its present location, opposite the Houses of Parliament.

Guy's Hospital is now located in St. Thomas's Street, and in one of the courtyards of Guy's Hospital you can see a stone alcove retrieved from the old London Bridge. It does not date from the 13th century but was designed and added by George Dance in the 18th century before Parliament ordered all houses to be removed from the bridge. Two similar alcoves are located in Victoria Park, Hackney.

After visiting the courtyard in Guy's Hospital, return to Borough High Road, and begin walking south. After only a few yards, you will discover Talbot Yard on your left, wherein used to be located the famous Tabard Inn mentioned by Chaucer in his *Canterbury Tales*, from which point his fictional pilgrims began their journey to St. Thomas's shrine in Canterbury.

In Newcomen Street, which adjoins Talbot Yard, can be found another remnant of the old bridge, in the shape of the Coat of Arms of King George II which used to be displayed over the gatehouse. They now occupy the most prominent place over the front door of the King's Arms although, at the appropriate date, they were amended to read 'King George III'.

At 77 Borough High Street you can find the George Inn, the last Galleried Coaching Inn in Southwark. At one time the galleried rooms used to overlook the yard on three sides, and coaches were turned around in the yard. Although in no way connected with either this Order or St. Thomas, it was frequented by both Shakespeare and Dickens, and so on that count alone deserves a visit.

Postscript

In fact, this whole area will justify a visit and, in addition to the landmarks relating to this Order, visitors can find historical reminders of the past in the shape of the Globe Theatre (a replica of Shakespeare's theatre), the Anchor Inn (from which Samuel Pepys watched the Fire of London), the Golden Hind (a replica of Drake's vessel), the site of Clink Prison (from which the word 'clink' is derived) and the Marshalsea Prison (which is where the family of Charles Dickens was incarcerated for debt), and the setting for most of Dickens' novels, such as the church of Little Dorrit, the back-alleys frequented by Bill Sykes and Fagin, and the Inn frequented by Sam Weller in the Pickwick Papers. There is even a pub (the Globe in Bedale Street) used during the filming of 'Blue Ice' (starring Michael Caine and Bob Hoskins) and 'Bridget Jones's diary' (starring Renee Zellweger), as well as the 'Tate Modern' Art Gallery, Borough Market (the oldest market in London, which can trace its origins to the market on old London bridge), and the new 'wobbly' bridge over the Thames (although it no longer wobbles).

The old London Bridge was a London landmark for over six hundred years and was not replaced until 1831. The new bridge lasted for less than one hundred and forty years and was eventually sold to the McCulloch Oil Corporation in the USA. It was re-assembled in Lake Havasu City, Arizona.

The walk described above is an 'easy' walk. There are no hills, but plenty of pubs and restaurants. Allow about three hours.

INDEX

	Page(s)
Acon Herald, The	12, 19
Acre, 1st Siege of	37, 38, 44
Acre, 2nd Siege of	47
Adhemar of Monteil, Bishop	28, 29, 31
Akko	4, 36
Ansell, K.	5, 6, 7, 56, 60, 62
Baldwin of Exeter, Bishop	24, 37, 42
Banner of the Order	18
Batham, C.	5
Becket, Agnes	22, 23, 42, 45
Becket, Gilbert	21
Becket, Mary	22, 23
Becket, Matilda	21
Becket, St. Thomas à	14, 15, 18, 21, 22, 23, 24, 42, 57
Bourke, Rev. D.	4, 7, 60
Bray, J. H.	56, 60, 62
Briwere of Exeter, Bishop	46
Canterbury, Cathedral	5, 13, 14, 19, 21, 57
Caritas, Knight	10, 19, 59
Chapels of the Order	64, 65
Chaucer, G.	67
Cheapside	21, 23, 49, 50, 66
Clairvaux, St. Bernard of	33, 42
Clarke, B.	5, 7, 10, 59, 60
Colechurch, Peter de	46, 49, 66
Colet, Dean John	3, 53
Conrad III of Germany, King	33, 34
Council, The Grand Master's	7, 11, 14, 15, 18
Crane, Bishop G.	7, 10, 11, 14, 60
Crusade, 1st	31, 32, 41
Crusade, 2nd	32, 33, 34
Crusade, 3rd	34, 35, 36, 37, 39
Cyprus	46, 47, 48
Diceto, Dean Ralph de	24, 43, 44
Duke, G.	5
Edward I, King	46, 66
Eugenius III, Pope	33

INDEX (CONTD.)

Gentry, G.	5, 7, 56, 60, 61
Grand officers	60, 61
Gregory VII, Pope	28
Gregory VIII, Pope	35
Harridine, M.	14, 61, 62
Hattin, Horns of	34, 35, 38
Helles, Theobald de	42, 45, 49
Henderson, K.	15, 16, 62
Henry II, King	21, 23, 42, 44
Hermit, Peter the	29, 31
Honey Lane	3, 52, 53
Hospitallers, The Order of	41, 43, 47, 48
Humilitas, Knight	10, 19, 59
Hussain, Sadam	34
Jary, J.	5
John I, King	39, 46
Kibble-Rees, D.	7, 11, 59, 60, 62
Lazarus, The Order of St.	41, 47
Leopold V of Austria, King	39
Loat, J.	15, 59, 60
Long, B.	59, 62
Lovas, A.	15, 16, 61, 62
Louis VII of France, King	33, 34
Lusignan, Guy de, King	36, 37, 41
Mitchell, J. W.	7, 10, 59, 60
Mercers, Livery Company of	50, 52, 53
More, St. Thomas	49, 53
Penrose, M.	5
Provinces of the Order	9, 63
Peter, The Hermit	29, 31
Preceptors, Grand	9, 17, 18, 19, 62
Raleigh, Sir Walter	30
Raymond of Toulouse, Count	28, 29, 31
Regalia of the Order	6, 18
Richard I, King	35, 36, 37, 38, 39, 44, 45, 57
Roche, Bishop Peter des	46, 67
Saladin	25, 34, 35, 37, 38, 39
S.R.I.A.	1, 2, 5, 7
Stephenson, A. B.	1, 4, 5, 7, 8, 56, 60
St. Nicholas Anglicorum	4, 47
Templar, Order of Knights	2, 6, 17, 38, 41, 55
Teutonic, Order of Knights	41, 44, 47
Tykehill, Sir Richard de	47
Urban II, Pope	27, 32

INDEX (CONTD.)

Walker, J. E. N.	2, 3, 4, 5, 6, 7, 22, 41, 56, 57, 58, 60
Walter, The Penniless	29, 31
Website of the Order	12, 19
William the Englishman	4, 24, 43, 44, 45, 57
Yong, Dr. J.	3, 51, 52, 53

www.ingramcontent.com/pod-product-compliance
Ingram Content Group UK Ltd.
Pitfield, Milton Keynes, MK11 3LW, UK
UKHW041434180426
11947UKWH00007B/436